Telyn has had enough. He only has his mother in his life — no friends, no family, no job, and no real future — but he can't stand the abuse anymore. He decides to leave his mother and life as he knows it behind, even though he doesn't have money or a place to stay, and heads for Gillham.

Lee's life is changing. He graduated high school, one of his best friends found his mate and moved in with him, and the other was arrested for helping a drug dealer with a kidnapping. Lee is also moving out of the house he's called home since he was adopted when he was eight, and he needs a bit of time to wrap his mind around everything.

So, of course, life throws him a curveball and drops his mate into his life. Lee has no idea how to help the demon he finds sleeping behind a dumpster, but he knows Telyn is his mate, and he's going to do everything he can to keep him safe and as happy as possible.

Things aren't easy, though. Lee throws himself into his relationship with his mate, but Telyn is much more hesitant. He doesn't know if he can trust Lee, not when he couldn't trust the one person who should have loved him unconditionally. Lee isn't easily dissuaded, though, and living on the streets weighs heavily on Telyn. They will have to learn to trust and to live together if they want a chance at a new beginning — for both of them.

Lee
Copyright © 2019 Catherine Lievens
ISBN: 978-1-4874-2518-0
Cover art by Angela Waters

Published by eXtasy Books Inc or
Devine Destinies, an imprint of eXtasy Books Inc

Look for us online at:
www.eXtasybooks.com or www.devinedestinies.com

Lee
Wyoming Shifters: 12 Years Later Book 8

By

Catherine Lievens

CHAPTER ONE

"It's gonna fall."

"No, it's not."

"I'm telling you, you're going to drop it, and then Lee won't want to talk to us ever again."

Lee rolled his eyes — *damn brothers!* "I already don't want to talk to you ever again. Why do you think I'm moving out?"

Lee had to admit he *was* slightly worried for the stuff Jamie was carrying. He'd decided it would be a good idea to balance a lamp on top of the two boxes he was holding, and Lee could too easily imagine the lamp shattering on the floor. He wouldn't care much, but their mom would, since she'd been the one who'd selected and bought it.

Jamie snorted. "We're just as relieved to see you go, ass-hole."

"Aww. Won't you miss my pretty face in the morning?"

"I'll miss having Brandon around more."

"We all miss him," Miles said as he snatched the lamp.

Lee breathed more easily. "He's not dead, you know," he pointed out.

"He might as well be. He's *mated.*"

"Not yet. Well, he and Maddox aren't bonded yet." Although Lee wasn't sure if that was because they'd decided to wait or because of the circumstances. He didn't think *he'd* want to bond, not after they'd lost Nathalie, but he wasn't Brandon.

God, just the thought of her and what she'd done made Lee so angry. And how had he not seen what was happening with her? He and Brandon had talked about it, and Brandon felt the same way. Lee thought Brandon had extenuating circumstances—a guy had drugged him and tried to rape him, then to kill him. And in the middle of that, he'd met his mate and moved in with him. And he was only nineteen.

Brandon made Lee feel like he needed to get his life under control, which was one of the reasons he was moving into his new apartment in Gillham, not far from the animal shelter where he and Brandon had summer jobs. Lee suspected Brandon would spend more time hanging from Maddox's lips than working, but then, *he* was probably going to coo over every single animal and try to take them home. Not that he had the space to do that, but maybe he could get a cat or something. Or he could go over to Maddox and Brandon's house and cuddle their pets. They had what felt like a dozen of them.

Miles waved. "They're going to do it sooner or later."

Lee arched a brow. "Do it? I didn't know you thought about them that way."

Miles' cheeks flushed. "That's disgusting. Brandon's like my brother. Hell, I like him more than I like you, and we *are* brothers."

Lee had been adopted, and having Jamie and Miles treat him like they were actually related always thrilled him. "That's because you don't understand the splendor that I am."

"Yeah, right. So, where do I put this?" He held up the lamp.

Lee looked around the apartment. It was furnished, thanks to Kameron and the pack, but Lee's personal stuff was still in the boxes he and his brothers had been carrying up the stairs for what felt like an eternity. "I have no idea."

"I'd personally put it into the trashcan," Jamie said. He dumped the two boxes he'd been holding onto a growing pile of other boxes. "That thing is ugly. Does Mom think we're still in the sixties? Lava lamps haven't been in since about then."

Lee shrugged. "I like it." He wasn't crazy about it, but he doubted he'd have a lot of visitors who'd see it, and the people who would come around knew his mom and wouldn't be surprised.

Miles pointed the lamp at Lee. "You're never going to find yourself a husband with this thing in your apartment."

"I don't want a husband."

"A boyfriend, then."

"I'm sure whoever I end up with will love the lamp." Lee didn't think he'd find someone anytime soon, though. He wanted some time to get used to this new life of his—a new apartment, one of his best friends in a serious relationship with their mate, the other one behind bars after betraying them for drugs. Sometimes, Lee wondered if he shouldn't have stayed home, where everything was familiar. He knew what to expect then, but he had no idea what tomorrow would bring him here.

"Lee?"

Brandon! Lee grinned, and Brandon appeared at the door a few seconds later, carrying four pizza boxes. Maddox was right behind him with two bags containing bottles, probably water and soda, since Lee hadn't yet gone grocery shopping. That was something he'd have to remember to do now, and he wasn't looking forward to it.

"Sorry we're late," Brandon said. He held up the boxes. "But we brought an apology."

"We should fight every day, if this is the kind of apologies you give," Jamie said. He made grabby hands, and Brandon handed him the boxes.

"Why don't you set up at the table? I think Mom put napkins in one of the boxes." Lee wasn't sure what box exactly, so hopefully he wouldn't have to open many of them. Of course, since his brothers were helping him move, he found the box labeled *kitchen stuff* in his bedroom.

"How are you holding up?" Brandon asked, startling Lee.

"Holding up? You make it sound like someone died."

Brandon shrugged. "Nat didn't die, but it feels a bit like she did, doesn't it?"

"I have no right to be angry with her, not like you."

"No right? Lee, she might have only put me in the hands of that drug dealer, but that doesn't mean she didn't hurt you, too." Brandon bit his lower lip. "And I know I hurt you when I told you I wouldn't move in with you. We had these plans, and I—"

Lee dropped the napkins back into the box and faced Brandon. "And you met your mate. I mean, you probably would have moved in with me if you hadn't stayed with Maddox when that dealer was hunting you, but it wouldn't have been for long. It's not like Maddox is just your boyfriend."

"Still. That doesn't mean I had to stay with him. We're not planning to bond anytime soon, and I promised you."

Lee shook his head. He wasn't sure why Brandon was bringing this up right now, although he supposed that not having Nathalie there with them was giving him bad memories. "I'm not angry with you. Why should I? I'm a bit disappointed, but trust me, you're not the one I'm angry with right now. I'll be fine on my own. Come on. We both know my mom is going to come around at least once a day to make sure I'm eating and that the apartment isn't turning into a dump. I'll be fine. Besides, we'll see each other every day, right?"

That was going to be the biggest change. They'd gone to school together most of their lives, and not going to school anymore was already huge. Not having Brandon right there with him was going to freak Lee out a little in the beginning. It had when Brandon was stuck in Maddox's house, and Lee had had Nathalie then.

He didn't anymore.

And he didn't want to think about her, because every time

he did, he got angry.

Brandon nodded. "Sure. That's why we both got a job at the shelter."

"That, and because I want to pet cute bundles of fur the entire day. You, on the other hand, probably want to pet Maddox's bundle of fur."

Brandon groaned. "That was so bad, Lee. Please stop making sexual jokes. I don't want to be unable to look Maddox in the face when we have to work together."

"You know I can't promise that. I have to make a pun when I see the opportunity."

Brandon smiled. "I'm glad to have you in my life, Lee."

"Same. Now let's go grab some of that pizza before my brothers eat all of it. I'm starving."

Lee didn't know what he would have done if he hadn't had Brandon when the Nathalie thing had gone down. Brandon had been there for him, even though he'd just met his mate. He wasn't going anywhere, either. Lee had realized that even though Brandon had Maddox now, it didn't mean he didn't have time or a place in his life for Lee. It would be different from before, but that didn't mean it wouldn't be just as good.

Lee would make sure of it.

Telyn was hungry, but he didn't want to leave his room. He wished his mother hadn't found the cache of food he'd accumulated over the past few months just last week. She'd been so angry he'd thought she would hit him. Instead, she'd taken the food and hadn't allowed him to eat for two days. Even now that he could eat again, she was only giving him bread and water, and it wasn't enough.

He rubbed his stomach and eyed his bedroom door. He could sneak downstairs to grab something, but his mother was home, and if she caught him, it wouldn't end well. She no doubt knew he was hungry, and he wouldn't have been surprised to find out she was spying on him, waiting for him to do something wrong so she could punish him.

He sighed and pressed the back of his head against the wall.

He hated his mother. He couldn't remember a time when she'd been nice to him. He didn't think that had ever happened, maybe not even when he'd been a baby.

"Dinner!"

Telyn jumped at the sound of his mother's voice just outside his bedroom. He *knew* she was spying on him. If he'd left his bedroom before she'd called for him, he probably wouldn't have been allowed dinner.

He didn't yell back. He knew better. Instead, he scrambled off his bed, straightened his clothes—even though he knew his mother would have something to say about the way he looked anyway—and went downstairs after stopping to wash his hands.

His mother was already sitting at the table eating. The TV was on, like always, and Telyn hoped it meant his mother wouldn't pay attention to him. The steak on her plate would help, too, even though its smell was making his stomach grumble.

He sat in his chair and looked down at the piece of bread on his plate. His mother was drinking wine while his glass was filled with water, but that was okay. He didn't like wine anyway. Her aura was its usual muddy green, so she wasn't angry—yet.

"You took your sweet time," his mother snapped.

Telyn was careful not to look at her. "I'm sorry, Mother."

"I sure hope you are. The next time you're late, you won't get anything to eat, so you better make sure it doesn't happen again."

Telyn nodded. He nibbled at the bread and did his best to

ignore the sounds his mother made as she ate. She groaned in pleasure every time she ate a bite of steak, probably on purpose. She always did.

Telyn reached for his glass. He knew the second his mother was going to do something because her aura flared. He heard her kick the leg of the table hard enough that his glass almost toppled over. He held his breath and wrapped his hand around it before it could, but he knew better than to think that was going to be enough for her not to get angry.

"You're so clumsy," she yelled, her aura flaring with dark red spikes.

"I'm sorry, Mother."

"You could have ruined the tablecloth."

"I'm sorry —"

"Oh, stop it. I hate when you call me Mother. It reminds me that I was responsible for bringing the waste of space that you are into this world."

The words would have hurt anyone else, but Telyn was so used to hearing them that they barely touched him. They'd already dug deep into his mind, leaving scars he wasn't sure would ever heal. This was just taking the scabs off, not digging the wound deeper.

Telyn's mother huffed. He knew she wanted him to lash out, to answer her. That way she'd have a reason to abuse him even more. They'd gone through this so many times that he wasn't sure why she expected him to do it again when he knew exactly what would happen if he did.

"My life would be so much easier if you were dead," Telyn's mother said. "I should have aborted you when I found out I was pregnant."

That wasn't new, either. Telyn continued to eat his bread. There wasn't much left of it, and he was still hungry, but he knew he wouldn't get anything else.

"You should kill yourself," his mother said, startling him.

That was something she hadn't said before. Telyn had suspected she wanted him to do something like that for a while, but he knew she enjoyed abusing him too much to allow it. Who would she berate and yell at if he wasn't there to take it? His mother didn't have friends, and they were each other's only family. The only people she saw outside of him were a few female demons she'd met through her job, like the mother of the man she'd wanted Telyn to marry.

"Did you hear me, Telyn?"

"Yes, Mother."

"Why don't you obey, then? My life would be so much simpler if I didn't have to think about you. I support you, make sure you have a roof over your head and food to eat, and I never hear a thank you from you."

The one reason Telyn didn't have a job was that she didn't want him to, just like he wasn't allowed to have friends or to leave the house. She was afraid he'd tell someone about how she treated him.

He'd never done that, because he doubted anyone would help him. He wasn't a child, so he had no excuse for staying there with her. Anyone he talked to about this would probably say it was his fault and that he was weak, just like his mother always did.

Telyn's mother made a disgusted sound. "Gosh, I hate the sight of you. Go to your room. And think about what I just told you!"

Telyn was relieved he didn't have to hang around until she was done to clean the kitchen. She usually made him do it and complained about how slow he was and how he needed to be more careful.

He didn't run out of the dining room, but it was a close thing. His mother's words twisted in his mind, coming again and again, always in her voice. *You should kill yourself.*

Maybe he ought to. His life as it was wasn't something

anyone would want to go through, not even him. The only thing the future offered him was years with his mother, listening to her insult him, letting her hurt him the way she'd been doing all his life. Sometimes, he wondered why he bothered to continue like this. Wouldn't he be better off dead? No one would notice except his mother. No one would care.

He closed his bedroom door and looked around for something he could use. Maybe the bed sheet? He could hang himself. Or a razor.

It was in Telyn's hand before Telyn even realized what he was doing. He snapped out of it and stared at the shining metal, dropping it to the floor as if it had burned him.

No. This was what his mother wanted, and that meant it was the worst thing he could do. He wasn't going to kill himself to make her feel better, to show her she was right about him being weak.

What other option did Telyn have, though? He couldn't kill himself, but he knew that sooner or later, he'd do just that if he stayed with her. His only way out would be to leave, and while the thought made him happy, he wasn't sure he could do it. Where would he go? He didn't have money. He didn't have friends. He didn't even have acquaintances. He didn't know anything outside of the home he'd grown up in and his mother.

Wait. That wasn't exactly true. He *did* know someone. They weren't his friends, far from it, but he'd met Felix and Nathan, and they'd seemed like good people. Nathan had even suggested Telyn go to Gillham if he ever needed something.

The thought was crazy. Telyn doubted either of the men would remember him, and even if they did, why would they want to help him? But maybe he could go to Gillham and see what happened. He didn't have to find Felix and Nathan. He could find a place to stay without reaching out to them. He wasn't sure how, since he didn't have any money, but anything would be better than staying with his mother for a moment longer, even if it meant sleeping on the ground and eating from dumpsters.

"I never want to see a box again," Jamie said with a groan. He reclined against Lee's new couch and pushed his hair away from his sweaty forehead. Lee tried to kick him, but he was too tired to do a good job of it. "Don't lay on my couch when you're all sweaty and stinky."

"I'll have you know I smell like roses even when I sweat."

"Yeah, rotten roses. Come on, man. I'll have to smell your sweat stink for the next month if you rub it into the couch."

"That's what you get for guilting me into helping you move, asshole."

"Do they ever stop?" Lee heard Maddox ask Brandon in a quiet voice.

He pressed his lips together. He knew Maddox well enough by now to realize he'd hate it if Lee put him in the spotlight by answering him. The fact that he was still there surprised Lee, but he was happy about it. He and Maddox were going to be in each other's lives for a very long time, so they needed to learn to be friends. Besides, Lee liked Maddox. He was a little weird, what with all those pets, but he was a good guy. He hadn't hesitated to take Brandon in when his life had been in danger, and they were in love. Lee only wanted his best friend to be happy, and that would happen with Maddox. It already had.

"We need to eat," Miles said.

"You're welcome to cook," Lee answered, gesturing toward the kitchen.

"I don't think I can move."

They'd worked all day, even though Lee didn't own that much stuff. But Kameron had wanted to make sure the apartment had everything Lee would need, so there had been a few furniture deliveries, and Lee had wanted to start emptying his boxes, at least the ones that contained what he'd need tonight and tomorrow morning. They'd also given the apartment a good cleaning, and Lee could feel the dust on his skin.

"We should go to the bar," Jamie suggested. "We can have a hot meal, relax, and of course, leave the bill to Lee."

"I haven't even started working yet," Lee protested. He did have some money saved, though, and he wouldn't mind offering dinner. His brothers and Brandon and Maddox hadn't had to help him, yet he'd never had to ask them to. He owed them at least dinner.

"Don't care. I want a burger."

They took turns in the bathroom to clean up and look at least presentable and not like they'd spent the day rolling around in the dust. Lee wanted to shower, but he didn't have time, so he just rinsed his upper body, generously applied deodorant, and hoped people wouldn't smell him coming.

Now that Lee lived in town, the bar was close enough that they could walk there. The air was warm, and people milled around, walking down the sidewalk even though it was the middle of the week.

They'd settled at a table in the bar when Lee's phone rang. He groaned when he saw *Mom* flash on the screen. He didn't want to answer, mostly because he didn't want to answer his mother's questions, but he knew she'd freak out. This was his first night away from home since he'd been adopted, the first night he didn't live there anymore, and he knew his mom would be a little maudlin about it.

"Order me a burger. I need to answer this," Lee told Brandon as he rose from his chair. His legs protested, but he ignored the pain and made his way toward the door. The noise from the bar faded as the door closed behind him.

"Mom?"

"Lee! I was starting to think you wouldn't answer."

"Sorry. We're at the bar to grab something to eat."

"You weren't feeling up to cooking tonight, huh?"

Lee could hear the humor in his mom's voice. "Nope. Besides, I don't think I should cook for five people the first time I do it on my own."

"You can do it if you focus."

Lee had learned to cook from his mom, but she'd always been there when he was in the kitchen, ready to save him if he did something wrong. She wouldn't be there anymore, not in the same way, and while Lee didn't regret moving out, it made him feel nostalgic. "I already miss home," he said with a sigh.

"And I miss you. But it's not like you moved to another town. You're only ten minutes away, and you know you can come home any time you want, even if it's the middle of the night. This will always be your home, Lee."

Lee had avoided this conversation for a while. He hadn't wanted to have it face to face with his mom because he knew he was going to cry. His eyes burned, and he scrubbed at them. "I know. I . . . you made it a home for me since the first day."

"That's all that matters. Did you go to the grocery store?"

"I didn't have the time." He was grateful for the change in topic. He leaned against the wall and looked around the parking lot, relieved to see he was alone.

"There's some food in one of the boxes. It's labeled."

"Food? Shit. I didn't think to check."

"Don't worry. It's cookies, bread, those kinds of things. I knew you might not think about putting it away in the fridge. There's also juice, so maybe put that in tonight. You can have it tomorrow morning."

"Uh, no. I'll have coffee tomorrow morning."

"No more than two cups, Lee. You're still growing."

Lee smiled. His mom was going to keep on mothering him even though he didn't live with her anymore. It felt good to have that certainty, to know he'd never be alone, no matter what happened. The thought of living on his own wasn't as daunting knowing that. "No more than two cups. Promise."

"Are you coming home on Sunday? We can have lunch. Actually, we should do that every week. I'm sure Jamie and Miles will leave the nest soon, too, and Sunday lunches will be my only opportunity to have all of you together."

"I'm in Gillham, Mom, not New York. But okay. I'll come by on Sunday and have lunch with you and the rest of the family." He didn't mind having somewhere to go on Sunday. Brandon would no doubt spend the day with Maddox, as it should be. Maybe Lee could go home for lunch, then visit them for dinner and watch a movie.

He wasn't looking forward to being on his own, even though he didn't regret taking this step. It was going to take him a little while to be comfortable with silence, but that was okay.

Something moved in the distance. Lee squinted, trying to see if it was someone he knew. He wouldn't be surprised, since more than half the pack came to the bar for a quick dinner or a relaxing evening with friends.

"You should probably go before one of your brothers eats your dinner," his mom said, distracting him.

Lee laughed. "They ate more than half the pizza we had for lunch just between the two of them."

"I suppose Miles has an excuse, since he's only seventeen, but Jamie is almost done growing."

"In his case, he's just rude."

Lee's mom laughed. "And not because I didn't try to raise him right."

"You raised us perfectly, Mom."

Whoever was in the parking lot moved again. Lee pushed away from the wall and walked that way, curious to see what was happening, especially after he noticed what he thought might be a tail. He only knew a few people with tails, and they were demons.

Was that what was in the parking lot? A demon?

"Call me if you need anything," his mom said.

"Sure. Bye." Lee was distracted now. He hung up and put his phone back in his pocket. He moved closer to where the movement had been. He was cautious and moved slowly, just in case he might startle whoever was there. He didn't understand what they were doing. They were by the dumpsters, but Lee couldn't see why.

There. There was a flash of movement again, and this time, he *knew* it was a tail. It was a pity it was dark, because he couldn't see much else. He didn't want to freak out the person who was there, though. He felt kind of creepy observing them the way he was, so he went back inside.

He couldn't forget that tail, though.

Telyn peeked behind the dumpster. It wasn't pressed against the wall like he'd initially thought. There was a space behind it, and from what he could see in the dark, the dumpster was blocked so it couldn't hit the wall. He wasn't sure why—maybe not to ruin the wall—but it didn't matter, not when it gave him a place to stay.

He was lucky it was summer. He'd have had a much harder time finding a place to sleep if it had been winter, but as it was, he managed to wiggle his way into the space behind the dumpster. He spread the blanket he'd brought with him on the ground. He didn't have a pillow, but he didn't think he'd be too uncomfortable. The ground was cleaner than he'd expected, as if whoever used the dumpster made sure the corner it was in stayed neat. Telyn hoped that since the dumpster was in a bar parking lot, it meant food would be thrown away. He'd stolen some money from his mother before leaving the house, but it wouldn't last him long, and he didn't want to use it unless it was an emergency. He had no idea what could happen to him on the streets, how or whether he'd manage to find a job and a place to stay.

So he had to think of the future, even though he didn't feel like he had one right now.

He settled on top of the blanket and pulled his backpack close. He didn't remember why his mother had bought it for him, but he'd been glad to find it in his closet when he'd decided to leave. He'd thrown some clothes into it, as well as some personal items like his toothbrush. He didn't know where he'd be able to brush his teeth and wash up, but he didn't have to figure that out tonight. He wasn't feeling up for it.

Telyn was shaken. There were no two ways about it. He'd never spent a night away from his mother. He'd never thought about a life without her. He'd known it wasn't possible.

He'd *thought* it wasn't possible, but here he was, without her. Alone for the first time.

Shit. What was he going to do?

Telyn's tail twitched. He was going to have to learn to wrap it around his waist like he'd seen other demons do. Humans knew about them now, of course, but apparently, they weren't comfortable with the visible signs that they were different. Or maybe the demons hid their tail for other reasons? Telyn had no way to know and no one to ask.

The realization hit him.

He was alone in the world now. He could go back to his mother, but he doubted she'd let him in the house, not now that she'd finally gotten rid of him.

What had he done? What was he going to do now? He'd never be able to find a job. He didn't know how to do anything. He didn't know anyone.

Telyn hugged his backpack and fought the urge to cry. He had to give himself time, but he couldn't see how that would make things better. He couldn't learn anything living on the streets. He didn't want to try to make friends and have to hide where he lived from them.

He wanted a home, a family, people who would love him the way his mother should have. That was why he'd left her.

Could he have that, though?

Being away from his mother was a good thing. There was no denying that, even though it meant living on the streets. Telyn was already less tense. He was still vigilant, because he had no idea what he might find here, but knowing he wouldn't be yelled at and insulted, that he could let his guard down at least a bit, helped him see he'd made the right choice.

A door opened somewhere close by. Telyn tensed, not knowing what to do. Should he stay still? Maybe it was just someone getting back to their car from the bar. The sound of music and voices was louder, then dimmed again when the door closed.

Footsteps came closer, stopping next to the dumpster. Telyn knew they couldn't see him, not from the front of the dumpster, but if they did, he wouldn't have a way to run. Maybe picking this place to stay hadn't been a good idea after all, even though it was protected and clean enough.

But no one noticed him. There was a bang that made him jump. His heart raced as he waited until he realized someone was throwing trash bags into the dumpsters. He slowly relaxed, but he stayed on his guard until he heard the footsteps move away and the bar door close again.

This was going to be his life from now on, and he had no idea what to do with it. Was he always going to be terrified of everything and everyone? How did he know who he could trust and who he should stay away from? Telyn had never felt so lost. He hadn't been happy with his mother, but he'd known what to do. He didn't now. He didn't know what tomorrow would bring, and that thought was terrifying.

But he wasn't a prisoner of his mother anymore.

Another door opened, more distant this time. There were more footsteps, and Telyn listened as the voices came closer.

"What else do you have to do?" a man asked.

"Empty the boxes. Actually, if you want to come around tomorrow night to help me . . ." another man answered.

Telyn put his backpack against the wall and moved to his knees. He peeked around the dumpsters and noticed a group of five men walking away from the bar. They were too far away for him to be able to read their auras, so he made sure to stay hidden.

One of them laughed, and when he spoke again, Telyn recognized the first voice. "I don't think so. And I don't think you'll want to do it, either. We'll both be too tired after our first day of work."

The man he was talking to sighed heavily. "Remind me why I agreed to work with you again?"

Telyn wished he could see more of him, but it was dark. What he *could* see was making his heart beat faster, though, and he wasn't sure why. The man was about Telyn's height, but he was wider—no doubt because Telyn hadn't been allowed to eat much in his life. The man looked strong and healthy. His skin was too dark to be tanned. The man's hair was dark, maybe black. It flopped in front of his eyes, and he pushed it back a few times.

Telyn wanted to do it for him.

Telyn shook his head. He had no business wanting to get to know this man or any of the other four with him. Who would want him, anyway? He was living on the streets now.

No one would probably want to talk to him, let alone get to know him and become his friend.

The first man wrapped an arm around the second one's shoulders. "Because you love me."

The second one laughed and pushed him away. "Shut up. You'll make your mate jealous."

Telyn had felt weird when he'd seen how close the two men were, but now that a third one grabbed the first one's hand and pulled him away, he felt better. He wasn't sure why, and he didn't want to examine whatever he was feeling.

He was no doubt out of sorts after what had happened earlier. It was no wonder his mind was trying to latch onto someone. Telyn had never been alone in his life, and he didn't know what to do with himself. He'd have to learn, though, because he never wanted to put himself in someone's hands the way he'd been with his mother ever again. He wouldn't give anyone that kind of power over him, no matter how cute they were and how much he wanted to see them smile from up close.

Telyn moved back. He wanted to continue watching the men, especially the one he found so pretty, but he knew better. He had to focus on his life, not on some guy he'd never see again. That was the only way he'd make it—and he needed to make it. He'd left his mother to find a better life, and that had already happened. He didn't want to stay on the streets, though, and that was going to take a lot of work to achieve.

He wasn't sure he was up for it. He wasn't sure he could do it. But he was going to try.

CHAPTER TWO

Lee wanted to adopt a pet.

He suspected it was more because he'd been working at the shelter for the past few days, surrounded by animals who didn't have a home, than because he needed one. It would be nice to go home to find someone waiting for him, though, maybe a cat.

"Don't even think about it," Brandon said.

"I don't know what you're talking about."

Brandon knocked their shoulders together. "Which one do you want to take home?"

Someone had dumped a litter of kittens in front of the shelter in a box during the night, and Brandon and Lee had been tasked with cleaning them up and feeding them. The vet would come around later to check them out, but they seemed to be okay. They were rolling around in the box right now, climbing all over each other and meowing. A red one was trying to get out of the box, but he was too short. Or was *she* too short? "I don't know."

"So you *were* thinking about taking one."

"Maybe? I mean, it wouldn't need as much care and attention as a dog, and it would be nice to not be alone at the apartment."

Brandon grimaced. "Not getting used to it?"

"Not yet. It's just weird, mostly."

"I could come around tonight."

"Don't you have something planned with Maddox?"

"Yeah, but we can do it tomorrow. He's not going

anywhere."

Lee had to smile at that. "Neither am I, and you know it. Spend the evening with Maddox. But maybe we can plan something for later this week?" He didn't need Brandon to hold his hand or anything, but it *was* weird to spend his evenings alone. He could probably call another of their friends if he wanted to go out, but he wasn't used to the work he was doing at the shelter, and he was usually exhausted by the time he got home. He was nowhere as comfortable with his other friends as he was with Brandon, so he'd rather not have them around his apartment when he crashed and burned at nine PM.

"Maybe you should think of a roommate. You have a second bedroom, and I don't think you'll have a guest who needs to sleepover anytime soon," Brandon suggested.

"Who would I ask, though? None of our school friends need a place to stay."

"Put up an ad?"

Lee shuddered. "God, no. Who knows what kind of freak I'd end up with? I'd rather get a cat at this point."

"As long as you read the stuff the shelter gives out before letting people adopt."

Lee rolled his eyes. "What, you think I don't know that it's a lifetime commitment? I've been hanging around your mate, Brandon."

"I know you know. Doesn't mean you shouldn't think about it long and hard, though."

The red kitten somehow had managed to hook his paws at the edge of the box and pull himself up. He had more trouble with the landing, though, and he tumbled into Lee's lap. Lee laughed and hauled him up until they were face to face. The kitten mewed.

Lee was done for. He was going to take this little guy—or girl—home, and he knew it. He'd still take a few days to think about it and buy what he'd need, but there was no way he wasn't adopting Red.

"You're a sucker for kittens. Who knew?"

Lee laughed. "Again, I've been spending time with your mate. If there's someone who's a sucker for animals, that's him. Has he tried to adopt anything else since you moved in with him?"

Brandon smiled fondly. "He brought home a rabbit a few weeks ago, but we managed to find her a forever home that wasn't ours."

Brandon always got all soft and sweet when he was talking about Maddox. It made Lee wonder if he'd be the same way if he met his mate. He hoped he would, eventually, but he wasn't obsessing over it. Still, it was hard not to at least think about it when he had Brandon and Maddox in front of him every day.

"Guys, what are you doing?" Asher walked in with a bunch of files in his arms.

Lee put Red back into the box. "We were just done with the kittens." That was a lie, and he was pretty sure Asher knew it, but the other man just smiled.

"They got to you with their cute little eyes and paws, huh?"

"Kinda."

"Okay. That's not a problem—you can come play with them whenever you want—but you *do* have work to do. Brandon, I need you to go clean up the kennels on the dog side. Lee, please take out the trash. Then you can go help Brandon."

Lee groaned, but that was why he was there, after all. Besides, he liked working with the dogs, too. They loved him when he threw them a ball.

He grabbed the box containing the kittens while Brandon headed to the dog side to start working. There was a kitten room—Lee's favorite room in the shelter—and he left the new ones there with the others. He kept an eye on them for a few minutes to make sure no one fought with anyone, but they all seemed to be okay with each other, and Lee had work to do. He snatched an adoption form on his way out, though, folding it and putting it into his pocket.

The trash had been stacked by the back door. There were several bags, and Lee could see a few of them were heavy just by looking at them. This wasn't going to be fun.

He propped open the back door and made sure it wouldn't slam behind him. Then he started hauling the bags outside. Luckily for him, the dumpster wasn't far, but it was still too far away for his taste. He dragged the first bag toward it and managed to raise it and drop it into the dumpster. He turned to get another one.

That was when he noticed the man sitting on the ground.

Not a man. A demon.

And he was asleep.

The demon had tucked himself close to the dumpster, almost behind it, and that was why Lee hadn't noticed him at first. Lee wasn't sure how the demon had managed to fall asleep sitting up, but he hadn't even reacted when Lee had dumped the first bag in.

Lee inched closer to get a better look. The demon was clean, cleaner than Lee might have expected of someone sitting behind a dumpster. He was wearing jeans and a t-shirt, and his tail was wrapped around his midriff, although the tip had flopped into his lap, maybe once he'd fallen asleep. It was pink, just like the swirls on the demon's skin. Lee could barely see them, because they were also pink and so pale they faded against his skin, but they were there. The demon's hair, on the other hand, was cotton candy pink, bright and happy-looking. His eyes would no doubt be swirls of black and pink, too, and Lee found that he wanted to find out if they were as gorgeous as he expected them to be.

He froze at the thought.

Why was he thinking that the demon's eyes would be gorgeous? Why did he want to find out who he was and why he was there, sleeping against a dumpster? What had happened to him?

Lee couldn't remember ever feeling so curious about anyone, guy or girl. Maybe that was because he'd always known his boyfriends and girlfriends before they dated, while the demon was an unknown. He was cute, and very much so, but that couldn't be the only reason Lee had to want to get to know him. He'd met plenty of cute guys, and he'd managed to never think about them twice.

He knew he'd think about the demon again and again, though. Maybe that was what pushed him to go even closer. He didn't want to wake the demon, but something in him needed to see him better. It was crazy, but he didn't see a reason he shouldn't.

Lee crouched in front of the demon, who didn't even stir. His long pink hair had fanned around his face. Lee reached out, ignoring the alarm bells going off in his mind, and caught a strand between his fingers. It was as soft and silky as it looked, and when Lee let go, he could smell the demon on his fingers.

He could smell his mate.

Telyn startled out of sleep, not knowing why. When he opened his eyes, he realized the reason. A man was crouching in front of him, reaching out for him.

Telyn scrambled to get away, but he had nowhere to go. His back was against the wall and his side close to the dumpster—a different one, because he'd had to leave the one by the bar when someone had come to clean the alley earlier that morning.

The man raised both hands. "I'm not going to hurt you."

Telyn's heart was racing. Was this man a cop? Was he going to arrest Telyn for sleeping in the street? He wasn't wearing a uniform, and he looked too young to be a cop, but what did Telyn know? "Who are you?"

"My name is Lee."

Telyn looked around. He needed to get out of the corner he'd backed himself into. He needed to be able to run away if he had to, and that wasn't going to be possible if he stayed where he was.

Lee seemed to understand that, because he got up and stepped back. Telyn thought he looked familiar, with his dark hair sweeping in front of his eyes, but he didn't give himself time to observe him. He got up, his back still pressed against the wall, and made sure to keep some space between them. He could probably leave if he went sideways, but he didn't have to, because Lee moved back again.

Telyn relaxed. Lee was still there, but he was far enough away that he wouldn't be able to touch Telyn if he reached out. He could if he jumped him, of course, but he didn't look dangerous.

Telyn finally gave himself the time to observe Lee and remembered where he'd seen him. He was one of the men from the bar the other night.

Telyn's voice shook when he said, "I'm sorry. I shouldn't have fallen asleep here. Please, don't call the cops." His mother might find out if Lee did. Telyn was twenty-two, so she probably wouldn't be called, but that didn't mean she wouldn't somehow find out.

"I won't call the cops. You didn't do anything wrong."

Telyn breathed easier. "Thank you." He turned to leave.

"Wait."

Telyn stopped moving. In truth, he didn't want to leave Lee. He wasn't sure why, and he didn't like the feeling very much, but he couldn't deny it. "Yes?"

"You didn't tell me your name."

"Why do you want to know?"

The corner of Lee's lips curled into a half smile. "I told you mine, and I'd rather have a name than continue thinking about you like the cute pink demon."

Telyn's skin was pale. It always had been, and that meant that when he was embarrassed or too hot, he blushed. Just like he was now, because no one had ever called him cute, not even his mother. *Especially* not his mother. "Telyn," he blurted out.

Lee's smile widened. "Telyn. I like it. Unusual, but it suits you. So, Telyn. Can I ask what you were doing sleeping out here?"

Telyn moved back. He didn't think Lee would hurt him, but he couldn't be sure. He didn't trust himself when it came to other people. He couldn't. He hadn't had a chance to learn people, and he didn't want to risk it. Lee's aura was promising, though. It was a nice yellow-green with hints of soft blue and gold — all good colors.

"It's all right," Lee said before Telyn could come up with an excuse. "I was just curious. I work here, you know? At the shelter. We just found a box of kittens. Maybe you'd like to come see them? They're adorable. I'm thinking about adopting one of them."

Telyn blinked. "Kittens?"

Lee huffed and rubbed his face. "Right. I'm babbling, aren't I? I'm sorry. I'm just not sure how to deal with this."

"With what? What's going on? I told you I'd leave."

"That's not what I meant, Telyn. Relax. I might work here, but I don't own the place, and I don't think anyone would mind you sleeping out here, although they might worry."

"They don't need to." Telyn couldn't trust anyone. He couldn't make that mistake.

"I don't think it's something you can stop. People tend to

be worried when they find someone sleeping behind a dumpster, but we can stop talking about this if you're uncomfortable, although what I'm about to tell you will probably make you even more so. I've been thinking about not telling you, but you have to know, and I guess I might be able to help you."

"What are you talking about?" Lee wasn't making any sense, and he was freaking Telyn out a bit.

Lee took a deep breath. "Okay, I know this is going to sound crazy, but I'm a shifter, and you're my mate. I know demons don't have mates, so you probably can't feel the bond, but I swear to you, I'm not lying."

Telyn wasn't sure what to say. It certainly wasn't something he'd expected to hear. "It's not possible." He didn't think Lee was lying—his aura hadn't changed—but his power wasn't precise enough for him to be sure of that.

"Why not? Like I said, I know you guys don't have mates, but shifters do, and you're mine. I'm sure about that."

"When did you get close enough to be?" The thought that Lee had leaned over him and had managed to smell him over the smells coming from the dumpster was creeping Telyn out a bit. He realized he'd probably be running away screaming if he didn't like Lee, though, and he couldn't deny he'd felt drawn to him since he first saw him in that parking lot. The fact that he seemed genuinely worried and confused only endeared him to Telyn even more, and that wasn't something Telyn could deal with, not right now.

Lee pushed his hands into his jeans' pockets. "Earlier, while you were sleeping. And I'm sorry about it. I shouldn't have. But you were there, so cute and sleeping, and my solenodon wanted to move closer."

"Your what?"

"Solenodon. My animal side. I'll show you what it is one day. Most people have never heard about them until I mention it."

It sounded like Lee was already planning for them to spend more time together. That wasn't going to be possible, though. "I don't—I'm sorry, but I can't do this."

"Do what? We're just talking."

"The mate thing. I can't be sure you're telling the truth, and I don't think you are. There's no way I'm anyone's mate."

"Why not? Not having a mate doesn't mean you can't be mine."

"Why would you want me to be your mate?" But Telyn knew why. Lee didn't know him, not the way his mother did.

He didn't know Telyn was a disappointment, that he couldn't do anything useful. He didn't know that Telyn had never gone to school and had never had a job. He didn't know Telyn was weak, useless, and a weight on anyone's shoulders.

And Telyn didn't want him to find out. A part of him couldn't help but hope Lee was telling the truth. Telyn wasn't sure why he'd lie, but he needed to think he was, because if he wasn't, that meant Telyn had something—someone. It would mean he could get off the streets.

But that would be taking advantage, and it wasn't something Telyn wanted to do. Besides, he had no way to be sure Lee wasn't lying. He couldn't trust Lee, no matter how nice he seemed. Telyn had seen his mother charm people and be friendly. She was a monster only with him, and the same might go for Lee, or for anyone else. No, Telyn was better off alone, at least for now. He couldn't trust himself to be able to tell if someone was a good person or not, and that meant he couldn't risk it.

"We don't choose our mates, Telyn."

Telyn swallowed. "I know that. And I'm sorry you were saddled with me. I . . ." He had to do this, didn't he? Even though he wasn't sure Lee was telling the truth. "I release you from the bond. I don't know how this works, but I don't expect anything from you. You can find someone else and be happy with them."

Telyn could leave now.

He tried to, but Lee stopped him again. "Wait."

Telyn sighed. He didn't want to do this. He didn't want to have to talk to Lee, to listen to him try to convince him to give him a chance. He *wanted* to give Lee a chance, but he couldn't, for so many reasons.

Telyn wasn't leaving yet, but Lee didn't know what to say to keep him there. He was panicking. "Do you live in town?" he asked even though he knew it was a stupid question.

Telyn blinked. "In town?"

"Yes. In Gillham." Lee suspected that Telyn not only lived in Gillham but that he also didn't have a place to go. There was no other reason for him to sleep on the ground.

The thought broke Lee's heart. Why was his mate living on the streets? Didn't he have a family? Or was his family abusive? Lee knew exactly how that felt, although he'd been lucky to be adopted by his parents when he was a kid. Telyn clearly hadn't had the same opportunity, and Lee wanted to help him. He wasn't sure how, though, and he doubted Telyn would tell him. He was wary, as he should be, since they didn't know each other. Living on the streets had probably taught him to be careful with strangers, and right now, that was what Lee was to him.

"I'm staying in Gillham, yes," Telyn confirmed.

Lee relaxed slightly. Gillham wasn't a big town, and it would make sense for Telyn to stick around Main Street. That was where the food places were, and he'd be less noticeable. Lee wasn't sure how to ask him if he was sleeping rough, but he wanted to know. "Do you . . ." He gestured at the dumpster.

Telyn's back went ramrod straight. "Do I what? Live here? On the street?"

Lee wasn't relieved that Telyn had realized what he was asking. It made him feel like an asshole when he was only trying to do *something* for his mate. "Yes. I'm sorry if I offended you, but I'm worried."

"Why should you be?"

Lee hadn't forgotten the way Telyn had spoken of himself. He hadn't gone into details, but it was obvious he thought little of himself — one more sign of abuse. It made sense that he wouldn't understand why Lee wanted to know if he was safe, but that didn't mean Lee wasn't going to push until he was sure of it. "I told you, you're my mate. Both me and my solenodon are worried. And even if you weren't my mate, I'd be worried. No one should live on the streets."

"Not everyone has a choice."

There it was. It was like Lee had suspected. "Did your family kick you out? Do you need a place to stay?" He desperately wanted to offer his own apartment and the guest room Brandon had pointed out was empty only minutes before, but he could tell that would only result in spooking Telyn and probably making him run. That was the last thing Lee wanted.

Telyn wrapped his arms around his torso. "You want to know where I'm sleeping."

It wasn't a question. "Yes, but I'm not going to push for an answer or details. I'd just like to help."

"No one can help me."

That sounded a bit too dramatic, but if Telyn had recently lost everything, it wasn't surprising. Lee didn't think Telyn had been there for long. He was clean, too clean to have been sleeping behind a dumpster for more than a few days. Maybe his wariness had nothing to do with sleeping on the streets and everything to do with the abuse he'd gone through.

Lee didn't know how to help him. He wanted to wrap

Telyn in a blanket and take him home, but he doubted Telyn would take that kindly. He didn't think Telyn believed they were mates, and Lee could understand that, if he put himself in his mate's shoes. An unknown man had smelled him while he was sleeping, then told him they were mates. Why should he trust Lee? Lee wouldn't have trusted himself in these circumstances, as much as it hurt to admit.

He took a step forward, but he made sure to keep enough space between them that Telyn wouldn't be spooked. "I only want to help you, I swear. You can believe or not that we're mates, but nothing is going to change the fact that we are and that I want to take care of you. I can tell you don't trust me, though, and that's okay. You will eventually."

That made Telyn smile. "You sound so sure of yourself."

"I wouldn't be if I were lying, but I'm not. Demons don't have mates, but they're not the only ones who don't. Humans don't, either, yet they can feel the bond. Not in the same way, and not as strongly as shifters do, but I know for sure that eventually, you'll feel drawn to me, that you'll want to get closer to me. You'll try to resist, and that's okay. But I'm still going to do whatever I can to make sure you're safe and as comfortable as possible, considering the circumstances. I *need* to do it."

Lee pushed his hand into his jeans' pocket. Unfortunately, he'd left his wallet inside his locker when he'd arrived at the shelter, but he had some cash. "Here." He handed the bills over.

Telyn didn't take them. He stared at Lee's hand, and Lee could see the conflict in his gaze. He probably needed the money, but what would taking it mean for him?

"I can't," Telyn finally said, his shoulder's slumping.

"Why not?"

"It's your money."

"You're right, it's mine, and that means I can do what I

want with it."

"And you want to give it to me?"

"Yes." Lee could only pray that Telyn wasn't going to use it on something like drugs. He didn't think Telyn drugged himself, not from his behavior, but then he hadn't realized one of his best friends was under the influence, and he'd grown up with her. He wasn't as observant as he'd thought. He wouldn't take the money back, though, not when Telyn might use it on food.

"I won't be able to give it back. To repay you."

"That's okay."

Telyn smiled. "Is it?"

"Yep. It's money. I'm not going to say it's not important, but you need it more than me. I can go back home anytime I want, eat with my family, and they won't say anything about it."

Telyn's cheeks flushed. "I don't—"

"Take it even if you don't need it. And if you're anxious about paying me back, we don't have to set a time limit on it. You can repay me next year, or the one after that. I don't care."

Telyn was still hesitant, but Lee was relieved when he snatched the money from him and pushed it into his pocket. "Thank you," he muttered.

"No worries. I wish I could do more."

"You've already done more than enough. I suppose you might not be lying about me being your mate."

Lee grinned. "I'm not." And even though he doubted Telyn believed it right now, at least he didn't think Lee was trying to trick him.

"Thank you."

"Don't think about it. And if you need anything, I work here at the shelter. You can come around and ask for me."

Telyn looked down. "I don't understand. I mean, I know you think we're mates, but we don't know each other. Even if

I am your mate, I could be a bad person. I could rob you and break your trust."

"You could, but I have to take that chance. It's not going to be easy to get me to give up on you, Telyn, not now that I know you. I'll do my best not to push, but I want you to know that whatever you need, you can ask me." Lee rooted around in his pocket, searching for a piece of paper to write his number on, but he couldn't find anything. "I want you to have my phone number. Can you wait here for a bit, just for the time I go inside to grab a pen and a piece of paper?"

"Why do you want me to have it?"

"Just in case. You can call if you need anything. I'll do my best to help, but I promise I won't push." It wasn't going to be easy to get Telyn to trust him, but Lee was stubborn. He'd chip away at Telyn's fear and distrust and get him to see what they could have together.

He wasn't sure when he'd decided he wanted to date his mate, but that wasn't going to change, and he'd make sure Telyn knew it.

It looked like he was going to have to wait to adopt Red. He already had more than enough on his hands as it was.

Telyn watched Lee turn and rush back into the building he'd come out of earlier. He wanted to wait, but why should he? He wouldn't do anything with Lee's phone number. He didn't have a phone. Besides, now he knew Lee worked at the shelter, so if he was desperate or needed anything, he knew where to find him.

He wanted to stay. He wanted to continue talking with Lee. But he knew this couldn't end well. He still wasn't sure he should believe that he was Lee's mate. He wanted to, but he couldn't see how it was possible. Surely Lee could do so much better than Telyn. He'd have to spend the rest of his life with his mate, and even Telyn didn't want to spend that long with himself. He could tell Lee would push, though, and he suspected he'd give in eventually.

In the meantime, he needed to protect himself and Lee.

He waited until the door closed behind Lee to leave the alley. He'd hidden his backpack under the dumpster, so he snatched it out, grateful Lee had left him alone for a bit. He wouldn't have been able to grab his things otherwise.

He snuck out of the alley after looking right and left. He wasn't sure why, since it was the middle of the day and people were walking around, but he knew it would take him a while to get used to living on the streets. He was still panicky whenever he thought about his mother, even though he knew she wouldn't be able to find him. How could she? He didn't have a cell phone, and he'd only been in Gillham once, to meet Felix, because his and Telyn's mother wanted them to date and get married. She wouldn't think to look here.

Telyn was hungry, but he didn't trust Lee not to follow him once he realized he wasn't in the alley anymore, so he went straight back to the bar parking lot. He stopped short when he saw there was someone by the dumpster there, though. He'd put his blanket back into his backpack this morning, so he didn't *have* to stay there, but he'd liked the tucked in space where he'd slept last night. He didn't want to risk being seen sneaking there, though, so he hovered at the parking lot entrance and watched.

He'd initially thought that the people there were the bar owner, or maybe the people who worked there, but the bar was still closed. That didn't mean no one was working inside, of course, and Telyn hadn't been there long enough to be able to recognize anyone.

One of the men kept looking around as if concerned someone was going to see them, and it got Telyn's attention. The other man didn't seem to either notice or care, though. He got something out of his pocket and held it out, but when the first man tried to grab it, he snatched it away and shook his head.

Telyn leaned a bit forward to get a better look. The second man was tall, and he looked like he could crush Telyn with his bare hands. His arms were bare, exposing tattoos on most of the skin there, including a prominent one of some kind of animal with its mouth open. Even from where he was, Telyn could see the fangs in the animal's mouth.

"Money first," the big man said.

Telyn was surprised he could hear him from where he was. He squinted, trying to see better. This man's aura was red, a color Telyn usually associated with power and force. It was tinged with a muddy brown, though, and some dark gray — violence, disgust, anger. Negative emotions. Telyn had seen this kind of aura on his mother often enough to know what he was looking at — and what might be about to happen. Not everyone with this color became violent, but the potential was in them, along with the anger to make it explode.

The first man patted his pockets for so long that Telyn thought he didn't have the money the big one was asking for. The big man's aura flared, hot and dangerous, but it simmered down when the shorter one made a sound of triumph and got a roll of money out of his underwear.

Telyn grimaced, but the big man didn't seem to care where that money had been. He grabbed the roll and eyed it. "Everything there?"

"Of course. Now come on. Give it to me."

The big man held out his hand again, and this time, when the other one reached for it, he let whatever he was holding drop into his hand. Telyn couldn't tell what it was from where he was, but there was a flash of something white, and it looked almost like it was contained in a small plastic baggie.

The smaller man peered at it, then put it into his pocket. The bigger one sneered. "What, you think we're not good for it?"

The smaller man's aura had been gray and muted until now, but it flared with dark blue — fear. The gray darkened, and the man took a step back. "Of course not. I know I can trust the Beasts."

"Good. See you next time."

The big man patted the other one on the shoulder so hard that Telyn saw the shorter man's knees buckle. He couldn't watch any longer, though, because the big one was coming his way.

He ducked behind a car, sliding down the length of it and holding his breath. He wasn't sure why he was hiding, but he knew he had to. Whoever this man was, he wasn't friendly like Lee, and Telyn didn't want to risk getting beaten or worse. He wouldn't be able to defend himself even from a child who might decide to kick his ass. He had no chance against the brick wall coming his way.

He slid around the car and crouched between it and the wall. He held his breath. He had no idea if this man was a human or a shifter, but he couldn't risk being heard breathing.

The man was tall enough that Telyn was able to watch him walk in front of the car he was hiding behind and onto the sidewalk. Telyn thought for a moment that the man was going to come his way and that he'd have to move again, but instead, he turned the other way and walked away.

Telyn breathed out quietly. He waited another five minutes before peeking up again. The parking lot was empty, and the big man was long gone, or at least Telyn hoped so. He got up, ignoring the way his legs protested, and carefully walked to the dumpster. He almost expected to be jumped or maybe punched, but no one was there.

He stood by the dumpster and peeked behind it. He'd decided to come back and hide, but after what had just happened, he wasn't sure he could stay there. He didn't know if it was safe. Well, it probably wasn't, considering it was in the back of a parking lot, but he'd felt safe enough last night. He hadn't fully realized what living on the streets had meant then, and he probably still didn't. He would soon enough, and that wasn't something he wanted to think about.

But it was summer, and the air was warm, the sun shining. Telyn didn't want to hide away for the rest of the day and the entire night. He was also hungry, so maybe he could use some of the money he had to buy a sandwich and spend some time in the park he'd noticed when he'd arrived last night. It looked pretty, and even though there were a lot of people there right now, he could probably find a quiet corner to spend the day.

Telyn got out the money Lee had given him from his pocket to count it while he was still isolated. He hadn't expected much—Lee had it in his pocket rather than in a wallet, and with how young he was, there was no way he earned much, especially not working in the shelter. But the twenty dollars Telyn was looking at would be enough for him to eat for a few days, more if he made do with only one meal. He had yet to look into the dumpster—he hadn't been able to bring himself to last night, even though he'd been hungry—but sooner or later, it would happen. Telyn wasn't looking forward to it, but it was the only way for him to survive, because he wasn't going back to his mother.

He'd rather die than do that.

CHAPTER THREE

Lee didn't know what to do.

When he'd come out of the shelter with his phone number yesterday, Telyn had been gone. Lee's first instinct had been to go after him, but he knew better. He'd freak Telyn out, and it wasn't like he could just walk out of the shelter. He could have told Asher and Maddox that he'd met his mate and needed to find him, but he didn't want to break Telyn's trust. He doubted Telyn would want anyone to know he was living on the streets, even if they didn't know him personally. Besides, Lee had talked to him long enough to realize how wary and scared he was. Whatever had happened to him in the past, it had made him timid, and Lee didn't blame him. He knew abuse and how hard it was to work through its consequences.

Lee wanted to do something, though. He knew Telyn lived on the streets, and Telyn was his mate. That meant Telyn didn't have to hide from him, although Lee suspected Telyn would anyway. He hoped Telyn hadn't gone far, because it would make it harder to find him again, but he wasn't sure that going out to look for him was a good idea. Besides, even if he did find his mate, what would he do?

Lee doubted Telyn would agree to move in with him, not when they didn't know each other. He would probably take one look at him and run away. Lee wanted to give him everything he owned, but he needed what he was earning to pay for food and whatnot and to build a small nest egg just in case. He still had no idea what he wanted to do once the summer was over.

Lee's phone vibrated, and he realized he hadn't answered Brandon's last text. Brandon was home right now, just like Lee was, but Maddox was probably at the shelter even though it was Saturday. Brandon and Lee only had a part-time job there, while Maddox worked full-time.

You're ignoring me, Brandon had written.

Then you should take the hint.

Asshole. What's up with you, though? You've been distracted since yesterday. Did something happen?

Lee hadn't told Brandon about Telyn, and he felt guilty about it. He didn't want to break the flimsy trust Telyn had in him, but he also didn't want to hide stuff from his best friend. Sooner or later, Brandon and everyone else would find out about Telyn anyway. *Something did happen.*

Instead of sending another text, Brandon called. Lee groaned. He wasn't looking forward to talking on the phone—a text explaining everything would have been so much easier and nicer—but Brandon wouldn't stop bugging him until he answered. It was them against the world now, at least when it came to their friendship, and they'd been clinging to each other more than before since Brandon had been betrayed and taken by Nathalie.

"Why are you calling me?" Lee whined.

"Because something is going on, and you won't tell me what."

"Only because you didn't give me time."

"Now you have it. What's going on?"

Lee bit his lower lip. "You know yesterday when I went to throw out the trash?"

"Yeah."

"There was a guy sleeping by the dumpster. A demon."

"Oh. You tried to help him, and he said no?"

Lee frowned. "Why would you think that?"

"Because that's how you do things. You always try to help

people. I imagine that if that man had been on the streets for a bit, though, he wouldn't trust you."

"He didn't trust me, but I don't think he'd been there long. He was clean, you know? But that's not all. He was my mate, Brandon."

Lee knew Brandon would be happy for him, just like he'd been happy for Brandon. He just wished they both could have gone through it more easily. Brandon's life had been a mess after he'd met Maddox, and only now were the two of them settling down in their new life. Would Lee's start with Telyn be as dangerous? Probably not, but he was ready to bet it would be just as complicated.

"Wow. I wasn't expecting to hear that when I called," Brandon said.

"And I wasn't expecting to find my mate sleeping on the ground when I took out the trash yesterday."

Brandon chuckled. "True. How do you feel about this, then? You're happy?"

"Yeah, I guess. I'm confused, mostly. I want to help Telyn, but I have no idea how, and even if I did, I doubt he'd let me. I think something happened to him to push him onto the streets. He's wary."

"Did you tell him he was your mate?"

"Of course. I'm not sure he believed it, though. I gave him all the money I had on me, but I don't know anything about him except for his name, not even where to find him. What do I do now, Brandon?"

"You have to earn his trust."

"I know that. How?"

"Why don't you talk to Kameron? He should probably know about Telyn anyway, and he might be able to give you advice, because I wouldn't know where to start since you don't know where to find Telyn. You should also tell your family, I guess."

Lee wanted to keep this to himself for a bit, though. His family would be over the moon, but they'd want to meet Telyn, and Lee doubted Telyn would be up for that anytime soon. "I'll talk to Kameron."

"I think he's here today. I saw Zach last night, and he was saying that Kam wants to spend more time with the twins this summer."

Lee didn't want to bug the alpha when he was home with his kids, but Kam was always busy, either with his family, his job as an alpha, or his job as a council member. It would be hard to find a moment when he didn't have anything to do, and Lee didn't have the time to make an appointment.

He headed to pack territory after hanging up with Brandon. Maybe he could go over to Brandon's house for lunch later. Then they could head into town to look for Telyn. Having Brandon there would probably spook him, but Lee knew he needed help.

Kameron was in the front yard when Lee arrived, playing with one of the twins. He waved Lee closer when Lee hesitated, then leaned toward his daughter to tell her something. She ran inside, not even looking behind, and Kameron sat down on the bench by the stairs and patted the empty spot next to him.

Lee had always looked up to Kameron. He'd taken him in when he was only a kid and had found him a family that loved him and had kept him safe since then. Most alphas wouldn't have even looked at Lee twice, but Kameron had protected him.

"I swear, there isn't a day that something doesn't happen around here," Kam said as Lee settled next to him.

"At least it's nothing bad this time?"

"It's not. I'm surprised. Maybe I shouldn't be, though. You've never been a troublemaker."

That was because Lee had been terrified he'd be kicked out if he was, but he didn't say that. He wasn't afraid of that anymore anyway. He belonged in Gillham. "I met my mate yesterday."

Kameron smiled. "That's good, although it makes me wonder why you kids are meeting your mates so soon. I didn't get with Zach until I was way past being a teenager."

Everyone knew about the age difference between Kameron and Zach and how old Kam had been when they'd finally bonded. "You knew Zach already, even though you didn't know he was your mate."

"I was still older."

"Zach wasn't, though, not by much. Besides, I doubt Telyn and I are going to bond anytime soon." Lee hesitated, but he'd come here to get advice. "He's sleeping on the streets. I don't know why or where, but he is. He's scared, and I don't know how to help him."

Kameron leaned back and linked his fingers over his stomach. "I see. What is he?"

"A demon."

"That makes things more complicated. He can't tell that you're mates."

"I know. I told him, but I'm not sure he believed me."

"I see."

Lee looked at his hands. "What do I do? I know I can't force him to trust me and I can't change anything by rushing, but I hate the thought of him sleeping behind a dumpster while I'm safe in my bed."

"You're right. You can't do much besides giving him time to trust you. That means getting to know him and showing him you *can* be trusted. I can't do that for you, but I can make things easier. Since he's your mate, I now consider him a pack member. You can tell him or not, your choice. I'm also going to give you funds to help him."

"I gave him some money yesterday, but it won't last long."

"That's why I want you to accept this. You know the pack has an account for this. We used that money to help you and countless others, and since your mate needs us, we won't back away. Just let me know when you need more and when he's ready to move somewhere. We can put together an apartment, food, and everything else he'll need."

Lee still hoped Telyn would move in with him when he was ready, but he knew he couldn't count on that happening. He was relieved to hear that he had the pack and Kameron behind him, though. It would make things much easier, both for him and for Telyn.

Telyn's stomach rumbled. He looked at the money in his hand, then at the bar. He'd noticed it was open for lunch, and he hadn't been able to stop thinking about eating since then. He didn't have much money, but it would be enough for a hot meal. Could he afford it, though?

The door opened, sending a cloud of sounds and scents toward Telyn. Even with the smells coming from the dumpsters, he could identify meat, potatoes, spices. His mouth watered and he swallowed.

He was doing this. He *had* to do this.

He checked that he'd picked up everything he'd taken out of his backpack. He didn't want to leave things behind because he didn't know if he'd be able to come back to the dumpster when he was done. He'd realized it would be better for him to spend his days in the park, because there were too many people coming and going in the bar and the parking lot during the day and the early evening. He didn't want to be noticed, and he knew his appearance didn't help with that. Humans and shifters didn't have pink hair, although he'd seen a pink-haired Nix the day before.

Telyn looked around to make sure no one was coming, then he rushed away from the dumpster and toward the bar door. He didn't know if he smelled bad, but he hadn't been able to change or wash up in a few days, so the thought of going inside made him cringe a little. He wanted a shower, but he'd have to make do with the bar's bathroom sink. Hopefully no one would realize what he was doing, but he'd have to be quick before anyone else could walk into the bathroom.

He realized he wouldn't be able to make a beeline for the bathroom as soon as he stepped in, though. He had no idea where the bathroom was, and the man behind the bar looked up when he heard the door. "Hello," he said.

Telyn licked his lips. He'd never eaten at a bar. "Hello." What was he supposed to say and do?

"You can sit wherever. I'll be right with you."

"Uh, thank you." Telyn looked around. His heart was racing for no good reason, and he tried to ignore it as he picked the empty table closest to the door. That way he could quickly leave if he needed to.

He put his backpack down on the bench only to snatch it up as soon as the man from the bar came closer. Telyn took a step back so they weren't too close—he didn't want the man to be able to smell him—and forced himself to smile. If the man thought Telyn was behaving strangely, he didn't say anything, not about that.

"I'm Nate."

Telyn frowned. "I'm Telyn."

Nate smiled. "Nice to meet you, Telyn. I don't think I've ever seen you in here."

"I'm, uh, new to town."

"That's nice. What can I get you? We mostly have bar food, so burgers, fries, things like that. We don't serve alcohol for lunch except for beer, but then, I'm not sure you're legal."

"I'm twenty-two, but water is fine." That was bound to cost

less than a beer, and Telyn had never had a beer anyway, and he wasn't planning that to change anytime soon.

Nate nodded. "Water, okay. And to eat?"

Telyn had no idea how much a burger would cost. He bit his lower lip, unsure how to ask without appearing rude or embarrassing himself. He couldn't come up with anything, though, so he just blurted out, "How much does a burger cost?" Then he looked at his feet. He could feel his cheeks heating, and he didn't want to see how Nate would react to his question.

"Five dollars."

Telyn blinked and looked up. "I'm sorry?" That couldn't be right. His mother often ate out, and she always complained to him about how much the food cost.

Nate's smile was gentle, his aura bright blue and gold—a sign he was generous and protective. "Five dollars."

"But—"

"Don't worry about it. So, water and a burger?"

"Yes, please."

"Good. Sit down, and I'll get this to you ASAP."

He turned to leave, and Telyn hesitated. He didn't want to bring more attention to himself, but Nate had been so nice that he wanted to make sure the bar wouldn't get a reputation of letting smelly people in to eat. "Can I use the bathroom?" he asked.

Nate smiled. "Of course. It's over there past the bar, in the hallway."

Telyn grabbed his backpack and nodded. "Thank you."

"Don't be too long. I'll have your burger ready in a few minutes."

Telyn rushed to the bathroom, relieved to find it empty. The main door locked, and he took advantage of it, hoping no one would come around for the next ten minutes. He used the toilet, then stood in front of one of the sinks.

He'd packed some soap when he'd left home, thank God. He took out the small bag where the soap, his toothbrush, and a few other things were and stripped his t-shirt off.

He never looked at himself in mirrors. He didn't like his reflection, the way the pink swirls were barely visible on his skin. They were a sign of his failure as a demon.

He used the soap on his chest and under his arms, rinsed it, then used it on his face and arms. Once that was done, he rinsed his upper body and used deodorant before putting on a clean t-shirt. He knew Nate would notice, and he hoped he wouldn't get kicked out of the bar.

He hesitated and looked at the door. No one had come knocking, so he probably still had a bit of time. He swallowed and took off his jeans and underwear. He'd have to put the jeans on again, but he had clean underwear. He quickly washed, used his dirty t-shirt to dry his lower body off, and put on fresh boxer-briefs and socks, then his jeans. He was pushing his feet into his shoes again when someone tried to come in. He rushed to put everything back into his backpack, his face feeling hot, then unlocked the door. "I'm sorry. I guess I locked it on instinct," he said without looking at the man who was trying to enter.

"That's okay. Don't worry. I just need to wash my hands."

The man's aura was a gentle indigo blue, but Telyn didn't linger. He went back to his table just in time to see Nate come toward him with a plate of food. There was already a glass of water on the table he'd chosen, along with a fork and a knife rolled in a napkin. He was still blushing when he sat and Nate slid a full plate in front of him, and it got worse when he realized there was no way all that food could cost only five dollars.

The burger occupied a full third of the plate. It oozed with cheese and ketchup and was filled with lettuce, onion, and tomatoes. The rest of the plate was filled with fries and salad, and Telyn's stomach grumbled at the smell. Still, he couldn't afford that. "I'm sorry, but—"

Nate shook his head. "Don't worry about it. I said five dollars, and that's all you're going to have to pay. We don't charge for water."

"But the food—"

"Eat, Telyn. You look like you need it."

Nate left, one of his hands on his back when his aura briefly darkened. Telyn didn't know what to say. He was embarrassed and ashamed, but he was also hungry, and that took precedence. He grabbed a fry and bit into it, moaning in pleasure at the salty crunchiness. He noticed Nate smiling at him from behind the bar.

Nate's aura was a nice one. It was made up of soft greens and blues, and it flared with affection when a man with long hair walked in from the hallway where the bathroom was. Telyn couldn't help but hear what Nate and the new man were talking about as they both worked behind the bar.

"Do you know how the guy we found last night is?" the new guy asked.

Nate shook his head. "I haven't heard anything, but then they wouldn't tell us about it. We're just the guys who found him."

The new guy scowled. "Yeah, OD'ing in the bathroom. I'm not saying you have a right to know, but it would be nice to be able to tell people no one died in the bathroom."

Telyn licked his lips. Someone had OD'ed in the bathroom. Was it that guy he'd seen buying drugs in the parking lot yesterday? Maybe he should tell Nate about it, but then he'd probably have to talk to the police, and they might want to know where he lived. He couldn't bring attention to the fact that he was on the streets.

He didn't know what he'd do if he couldn't stay there.

Lee tried to relax, but his thoughts were never far from Telyn.

"You want to go to him," Brandon said.

"Yeah. Is this how you feel about Maddox?"

Brandon smiled. "Pretty much, I guess."

Lee groaned and pressed the back of his head against the couch. "Damn. It's like I can't stop worrying about him."

"Well, your case is different. I mean, I worry about Maddox, but the worst that can happen to him is that he'd get bitten by a dog or something. Your mate is homeless, so it's no surprise you're obsessing over his safety, especially with the Beasts in town."

Lee hadn't thought about that, and now he felt even worse. He wanted to drag Telyn off the streets and into his apartment and make sure he was safe and fed and everything else, but he couldn't. He might not know Telyn, but he could tell that would freak him out and maybe push him away from Gillham. Then Lee wouldn't be able to find him, and that was the last thing he wanted.

Brandon poked Lee's leg with his foot. "What did Kameron say?"

"That he considers Telyn a pack member. He gave me some money to buy him food and whatever he might need, and he told me that once Telyn was ready, the pack would take care of finding him a place to stay."

"That's great."

"Yeah. Doesn't help me be less worried. I hate to imagine him sleeping behind the dumpster tonight, you know? I mean, it's probably stupid because it's not me sleeping there, but I'm worried."

"Of course you are. You haven't seen Telyn today, right?"

"No. I looked around when I left my apartment, but I didn't find him."

"Why don't we go into town? We can grab some food for

him, maybe stuff that will keep until he needs it."

"I don't think he'd be happy to see you. No offense, but he was already freaked out when it was only me."

"That's okay. I want to help him, not to push him and make him uncomfortable. But I can help you look for him." He sat up, crossing his legs. "Look, you're worried, and that's understandable. You also need to get to know him better, because he's never going to trust you if he can't see how good of a man you are and that you're not going to hurt him."

"You think I'm a good man, huh?" Lee wasn't too sure about that. He wasn't a bad one, but most days, he still felt like a kid. Living on his own had helped with that, but it was only the first step. He was only nineteen, so he had time, but meeting Telyn made him want to grow up now because that was the only way to help him. Lee needed to become responsible and steady because his mate needed him—and because he wanted to. Brandon was leaving him in the dust when it came to that, and Lee had always been competitive. Besides, he didn't want his best friend to grow up without him. He wouldn't be able to stand losing someone else, even if it was only because they drifted away.

Brandon patted Lee's knee. "I'll leave as soon as we find him, okay? You can tell him about me so he'll know who I am and that he's going to see me again, but I won't intrude. You have to earn his trust, and pulling me into this won't help with that. But I still want to be there for you and to help you look for him. It'll be easier if there are two of us."

"All right." Lee could use the help.

Maddox wasn't home, so Brandon had to put the dogs into their crates and check on the other pets before leaving.

Lee found it amusing—Brandon had never had a pet before he'd moved in with Maddox, and he cooed and talked to them as if they were children. "They're not kids," he teased once Brandon was done and they were in his car.

"I know they're not, but Maddox loves them. So do I."

"Are you planning on adopting a few more now that there are two of you to take care of them?"

"Gosh, no. I love them all, but some nights, I can't even touch Maddox because the cats are sleeping between us. And that's when we remember to put the dogs in their crates. The other night, we fell asleep on the couch, and when we went to bed, they were all there. There wasn't a spot for us anymore."

Lee chuckled. "You do have a lot of them."

"Yeah. Mom's not happy about it. She never visits, although that might be more because she doesn't like that I live with Maddox."

"She's still angry about that?"

"Yeah. She thinks I'm too young to move in with my boyfriend."

"But Maddox isn't just your boyfriend. He's your mate."

"I think she's terrified we'll decide to bond soon."

"Because she thinks you're too young."

"Yeah."

It made sense in a way. Brandon was nineteen, like Lee, and Lee didn't even feel close to being ready to make that big a commitment. But on the other hand, Brandon and Maddox were mates. That meant they already knew they were going to spend the rest of their lives together, and when they bonded didn't matter. Hell, they'd gone from not knowing each other to living together over the space of a few weeks — and Lee wasn't counting the time Brandon had spent at Maddox's house because a guy was trying to kidnap him. But Brandon was happy, and that was all that mattered. Everything else was between him and Maddox, and Lee trusted Brandon to tell him or someone else if something was wrong. He was old enough to make his own decisions, although Lee supposed it was easier to accept that as Brandon's best friend than as his mother.

He parked at the grocery store, and he and Brandon went inside. Lee had no idea what to buy—Telyn couldn't keep a lot with him, since he only had a backpack, and it had to be things that didn't need to be refrigerated.

"How about some bread? Maybe cookies?" Brandon asked. "I know it's not exactly nutritious, but it'll do if he doesn't have the opportunity to go somewhere to eat, and it'll keep well."

Lee wanted to stuff Telyn full of vegetables and meat—he was way too thin, and living on the streets wasn't going to help.

"Where to now?" Brandon asked when they left the store.

"I don't know. He was behind the shelter when I met him."

"Let's head that way, then."

They didn't get that far, because Brandon stopped in front of the bar. "You said your mate's hair is pink?"

"Yep."

"Is that him?" Brandon tilted his chin toward the door of the bar.

Telyn was coming out of it, his cheeks flushed, wearing different clothes from the ones he'd had on yesterday. He looked just as gorgeous. His skin was so pale that he glowed in the sunlight. He closed his eyes and tilted his face toward the sun. The gesture made Lee's heart hurt in a good way. He wanted to wrap his arms around Telyn and protect him from the world, but since he couldn't do that, he'd have to be satisfied with feeding him.

"I'm going to go back to the car, okay?" Brandon said.

"Yeah, okay."

"Just . . . keep calm, and don't push him. We don't know what happened to him, but since you think someone abused him, he's going to need time."

"I know." Lee could remember that all too well. He just hoped that being an adult would mean Telyn would trust more easily. Lee couldn't even think about what might happen if he was still living on the streets when winter came.

"You can do this, Lee. Telyn is your mate. No matter how scared and wary he is, that will mean something to him."

"He's a demon. He doesn't have a mate."

"Maybe not, but he's yours. He'll feel it eventually if he doesn't already. It might not be as strong as if he were a shifter, but it's there. It always is, even with humans. Just give him time to wrap his head around everything. You said he was new to sleeping out here as well, right?"

"I think so."

"Then it's a lot to deal with. I know it's hard. I can't even imagine what it's like, but I see how torn you are over this. Give him time."

That was going to be the hardest part of this. Lee wanted to help his mate, but he couldn't, not until Telyn was ready to accept it.

"Telyn."

Telyn jerked at the sound of a voice so close to him. He opened his eyes, relieved to see it was Lee. He might not trust Lee entirely, but he didn't think he was there to hurt him. "What are you doing here?"

Lee held up the bag he was holding. "I brought you something."

Telyn blinked. "What?" He hadn't expected that. He'd known he'd see Lee again—Lee thought they were mates, and he was probably right about that. That meant he was drawn to Telyn and that he wanted to help him. It *didn't* mean Telyn could trust him, no matter how much he wanted to, but Telyn was ready to give him a chance.

Lee shrugged. "It's just some food. Stuff you can keep in your backpack."

Telyn wasn't sure what to say. He was kind of choked up already after what Nate had done for him, letting him pay only five dollars for that burger. Telyn had never felt so full, and now Lee was there, offering him more food, and he didn't know how to deal with it.

"Telyn?" Lee's voice was gentle, and it broke something inside Telyn.

No one had ever been gentle with him. The only person he'd spent time with had been his mother, and she'd treated him as if he were disgusting, someone not worth caring about. The fact that two people he barely knew cared more for him than his own mother had was something Telyn didn't understand, and that he had a hard time processing.

"Why don't we go sit down in the park?" Lee asked. He sounded careful and a bit alarmed, and Telyn realized this had to be an odd situation for him.

Telyn cleared his throat. He still felt too touched to speak, but he didn't want to annoy Lee. "If you have time."

Lee smiled. "I wouldn't have asked if I didn't, and let's be honest — I'll always have time for you."

"I really am your mate, aren't I?" Telyn asked once they were walking toward the park. He couldn't remember a time when he'd felt so good. His back hurt a bit because he'd spent the past two nights on the ground, but he wasn't hungry, the sun was shining on his face, and he was walking with Lee. He still didn't know if he could trust him, but he was inclined to. Not enough to go with him if he tried to convince him to. Telyn wanted to sleep in a bed, but not enough to take that risk, not yet.

"What did you want to talk about?" he asked when they reached one of the empty benches. There were a lot of kids running around, some of them followed by a lion, and Telyn couldn't look away. Demons were used to hiding in their towns, where everyone was a demon. He'd never seen anything like this. The humans around — not that he could tell who was a human and who wasn't — didn't seem to mind or be afraid. They knew it was a shifter, of course, but that didn't change the fact that it was intimidating as hell, and scary.

Lee handed the bag to Telyn again. "It's not much, but I wanted you to have something, just in case you need it."

Telyn took the bag — he couldn't afford *not* to, and he didn't want to offend Lee — and peeked into it. Lee might think it wasn't much, but it was everything to Telyn. There were cookies and crackers in it, as well as wet wipes and deodorant. There was even a loaf of sliced bread and some cold cuts.

"The meat is for tonight. I guess I thought you might want to eat, but I didn't think to ask if you eat meat. I can buy you something else if you don't."

"This is perfect."

"Are you sure? I know it's not much, and I pretty much picked whatever *I'd* eat."

"It is. Thank you, Lee. I didn't expect this, and I'm grateful." Telyn's cheeks flushed. "And thank you for the money you gave me yesterday. I bought lunch at the bar today."

"Yeah? What did you get?"

"A burger. Nate only made me pay five dollars, and I know that wasn't right. I hope he won't get in trouble."

"Nate's good guy, and he'll be fine. He's the owner, you know."

Telyn hadn't, but it made him feel better. "I don't know why you and Nate are being so nice to me. I don't understand it."

Lee sighed and leaned back against the bench. "Well, I don't know about Nate, although he's genuinely a nice guy. He'd try to help you if you told him what's happening with you, but he'll never push. I know you're not comfortable telling me or probably anyone else what happened to you and that you don't trust anyone, but if you ever need anything, you can go to Nate. He'll take care of you, and he won't ask anything in return." Lee grinned. "And just so you know, I snuck my phone number into that bag."

"I didn't mean to run yesterday."

"Yeah, you did, but that's okay. I get it." Lee hesitated. "I've been where you are. It wasn't the same situation, but I can understand not knowing who you can trust and not being able to count on anyone but yourself. You're doing a good job, but no one can live on their own for long. We all need people in our life, friends or even only acquaintances. It's going to take you time to see that and to trust me, but I'm not going anywhere."

"Because I'm your mate."

"That, and because like I said, I get it. I had a shitty start in life, but I found people who love me and whom I love back, and now I'm happy and safe. You can have that, too, in time, if you let yourself see that not everyone is like whoever hurt you."

Telyn wasn't surprised Lee had realized why he was on the streets. He didn't want to talk about it, though, and he didn't want to hear Lee's tales about how he'd gotten hurt. It would remind him of too many times his mother had abused him. "You said you found people to love?" he asked.

Lee grinned. "Yeah. I was adopted when I was eight. Kameron, the pack's alpha, brought me here and helped my parents."

"He didn't care that you're not a wolf shifter?"

"Nah. Kam doesn't care about any of that. Just look at the pack. We have wolf shifters, of course, like my family, then there are humans, a few demons, hell, even a shark shifter. No one cares as long as you're good people and you follow the rules." He bit his lower lip. "Actually, I told him about you this morning. I needed some advice."

Telyn's stomach churned. The alpha couldn't kick him out

of Gillham since it wasn't pack territory, but he could make his life harder. "What did he say?"

"That since you're my mate, you're also a pack member. He understands you might be wary, though, and he's leaving everything to me. But if you'd rather talk to him, you can. You just have to say the word. I know you don't trust me, and that's okay. I just want you to feel safe enough that you'll eventually accept help."

"Why would the pack do that?"

"That's how Kameron is. The pack wasn't always welcoming and accepting, and he's been changing that ever since he became the alpha. He doesn't care who you are, what happened to you, as long as you're a good person, and I think you are."

Telyn wanted to say yes. He'd never dreamed something like this could happen when he'd decided to leave his mother's house. He wasn't made for life on the streets, but then who was? He knew he wouldn't be able to stay there for long, but how could he trust someone he didn't know? "I'll think about it." His freedom was the most important thing right now. He couldn't risk it.

He couldn't trust his mother, and she was the one person who should love him and protect him. He wasn't sure he'd be able to trust anyone else.

"That's fine. I'm not going to force you to do anything. No one is. But living on the streets can be dangerous, and I need you to be safe. I know it doesn't make sense to you."

"It's because of the mate bond."

"In part. But I wouldn't be happy about anyone being homeless. I can't deny I feel especially protective of you, though. I want you to be safe and happy, and eventually, I hope you'll realize I'm not lying. But if you want to stay where you are, remember to stay around Main Street and to either call me or go to the bar if anything happens. Please."

Telyn had already seen where the police station was, but it was nice to know he had alternatives if he needed them.

He hoped he wouldn't, though. Life on the streets was already rough as it was, and he didn't need it to get rougher.

CHAPTER FOUR

L ee didn't know what to do. He'd first met Telyn a few weeks ago, and he still hadn't had any luck convincing him to move into an apartment. He didn't even care if it was his or one of the places the pack owned in Gillham. He just wanted Telyn off the streets.

There had been another OD last week. That was the second one since Telyn had arrived in town after the guy who'd OD'ed in the bar's bathroom, and fear gripped Lee's stomach every time he thought about his mate. Someone was dealing drugs in Gillham, and everyone knew it was the Beasts.

No one had managed to do anything about it yet, though, and Lee wasn't hopeful. Knowing the Beasts were behind it was both terrifying and unhelpful. No one had any idea who belonged to the Beasts, and while most of the gang members bore their gang's tattoo, they were good at keeping hidden. As far as Lee knew, no one but the people buying the drugs knew who the dealer was, and that was complicating the police investigation. They couldn't even get the people who were still alive after their OD to talk. Everyone's mouth was sealed shut because they knew they wouldn't be alive for long if they opened it.

So no one could do much about the Beasts, and Telyn was still out there, living behind the bar. Lee hated that, but he hadn't pushed, not yet. He understood where Telyn was coming from.

He wouldn't be able to keep his distance for long, though. He'd been bringing Telyn food every few days since they'd met, and things were more relaxed between them. Lee found that he wanted to drag Telyn to safety, but he knew that would destroy all the trust Telyn had in him. He was starting to wonder if it wasn't worth it, though. He'd have to start from the beginning again if he did it, and Telyn might not want to talk to him again, but at least he'd be safe.

Lee sighed and rubbed his face. He'd been thinking about this for the past week, and he still didn't have an answer. He didn't think there was one, not a good one anyway. That was why he didn't know what to do.

He slapped the slice of bread he was holding onto the sandwich and wrapped it, adding it to the bag where the other two sandwiches already were. He was meeting Telyn in the park in a bit, so he needed to get a move on.

Fear aside, things were going well between them. Telyn was still wary, but Lee knew that living on the streets was weighing on him, and they'd talked enough times now that he knew Lee wasn't going to hurt him—or at least Lee hoped so. They'd talked about pretty much everything in Lee's life, from his job to his family and even Brandon, but he still knew very little about his mate. He had no idea why Telyn was living on the streets or what waited for him at home if he ever went back. He wasn't sure he wanted to find out, because just the thought of someone hurting Telyn made all his protective instincts—which he hadn't realized he had—flare up.

He was falling in love with Telyn. There were no two ways about that. Telyn was sweet, and while he looked fragile, he'd been brave enough to leave whatever life he'd had before even though he hadn't had a place to stay or friends to help him. That took a lot of guts, and Lee was in awe every time he thought about it. Telyn was also fun when he relaxed enough to let go of his tightly held control. He wasn't a talker, but he listened to every word that came out of Lee's mouth. Lee's days were always brighter when he got to spend time with his mate, and he looked forward to those moments.

Lee had bought other things for Telyn, mostly wet wipes and a few bars of chocolate, because he'd found out Telyn had a sweet tooth a mile wide, and he packed those, too. He was looking forward to their date. Telyn always blushed and got flustered when Lee gave him stuff, even though it was always food and necessities, and it was endearing. It made Lee want to buy a lot more stuff for him, but he knew Telyn wouldn't take it well. He could see how hard it was for him to accept food and money sometimes, and he didn't want to push so hard that Telyn would close himself off.

Telyn was already waiting for him at what had become their bench. He was sitting there, his arms wrapped around his backpack as he looked at the people walking past him. He was always guarded when it came to strangers. When he noticed Lee, Lee smiled and waved at him, grinning even wider at the sight of the blush on Telyn's cheeks.

"I brought lunch," he said, holding the bag up.

"You didn't have to."

Lee shrugged. "Why not? We both need to eat, don't we?" He'd found out that Telyn was less reluctant to accept food if he ate with him, so he'd started making sandwiches and whatever other food he made for both of them. "And I'd rather have lunch with you out here than alone at home."

"You still miss your family."

"Yeah." Lee flopped onto the bench. "It's gonna take me a while to get used to not having them around, especially my mom. She's the best cook, and I can't compare to her." He dug into the bag and handed Telyn one of the sandwiches.

Lee had observed Telyn over the past weeks, so he had a good idea of what Telyn liked and didn't like to eat. The sandwich was simple—mayo, turkey, lettuce, and tomato—but Telyn's expression was pleased when he unwrapped it.

Telyn was usually silent when they were together. He

answered most of Lee's questions unless they were about his past, but he always looked like he wasn't quite sure what to do if Lee didn't take the first step. "So, what do pink demons do?" Lee asked. He'd been dying to find that out since the first time he'd seen Telyn. "I know a bit about orange demons, and we also have a blue and a green one in the pack, but I've never heard about pink ones."

Telyn grimaced and put the sandwich down. "That's because we're useless."

Lee blinked. "What?"

Telyn shrugged. "We see auras. It's kind of like being empaths, but auras are harder to read, and my power is especially weak."

"I think that's cool."

Telyn's head jerked up. "You do?"

"Yeah. I'll be honest, the thought of someone who isn't my mate being able to read my emotions freaks me out a little. Auras seem to be more, I don't know, like an expression on my face or something."

"But it's useless."

"Why? I bet you'd do a great job working with kids. You'd be able to tell how they feel without having to push them to talk."

Telyn stared at Lee. Lee suspected he'd never thought about the ways he could use his demon powers. He seemed so focused on how few of them he had and what he couldn't do that he'd probably never thought about what he *could* do.

Lee leaned closer. "Humans don't have powers, and they have perfectly good lives."

Telyn looked at his half-eaten sandwich. "But I'm not human."

"So? Whatever you can or can't do doesn't reflect your worth or who you are, Telyn. I don't care about your powers, and no one in their right mind would. I like you for you, not for what you can do with the auras."

Telyn's head snapped up. "You like me?"

"I thought I'd been obvious about it."

"Not for me. I'm not used to this."

"To having someone in your life?" Lee didn't think Telyn had ever had a boyfriend, but he couldn't be sure without asking.

"To having someone in my life who isn't yelling at me because of what a waste of air and space I am." Telyn's voice was soft, but Lee heard him anyway.

"You're *not* a waste of anything," he said. He didn't want to spook Telyn with how angry he was, but damn. He wanted to strangle whoever had hurt his mate that way.

To Lee's surprise, Telyn smiled at him. "I'm starting to believe that, and it's thanks to you."

It wasn't often that Lee was speechless, and Telyn had a hard time believing he'd been the one to manage to get him to be quiet. "Lee?" he asked. He was smiling, and he couldn't seem to stop.

Lee blinked. "Sorry. I just didn't realize you felt this way. I've been praying that you'd start to trust me, but . . ."

And now Telyn felt guilty. He knew Lee was doing everything he could to make him see he was a good man, and he wanted to believe that. He wasn't sure he could, though. The thought of trusting someone, even Lee, was petrifying, and Telyn didn't think he was ready to take that step. The thought of what could happen if he trusted the wrong person was too scary. He never wanted to feel like he'd felt when he was with his mother again, and while Lee had been nothing but understanding and kind with him, things could change. *People* could change.

Telyn wanted to believe he could trust Lee, though. He

couldn't deny they were mates anymore, not with the way he felt about him. He'd never felt drawn to anyone else the way he was to Lee. Maybe that was because he hadn't had the opportunity, but he didn't think so. And with the way Lee treated him, how he always made sure he had food and whatever else he needed, Telyn knew Lee was just as drawn to him. No one would behave the way he was otherwise.

They were mates. That meant Telyn could trust Lee. He realized that being Lee's mate didn't make Lee a good person, but he was. Telyn had observed him long enough to know that, and auras didn't lie. Lee's auras told Telyn that he was a creative man, a man who was truthful and intuitive, who would protect him.

"I wish you'd agree to move into one of the pack's apartments," Lee murmured.

"I might." Because Telyn was sick of living on the streets. It was hard, and he hadn't felt safe ever since he'd arrived in Gillham. He saw that man with the tattoo everywhere he went, or at least, that was what it felt like. He knew about the people OD'ing, and while he'd been isolated most of his life, he was pretty sure the man with the tattoo was a dealer. He knew he had to do something with the information he had, but what would happen if he went to the police? Would they call his mother, or maybe arrest him because he was living on the streets?

He wasn't hungry anymore. He wrapped the rest of his sandwich and put it into the bag. "I should go back." Lee knew he slept behind the dumpster at the bar, so Telyn could be honest with him.

"What's wrong?"

"Nothing." Telyn felt guilty. Lee and the pack were helping him as much as he let them, yet he knew something that could help them, and he hadn't told anyone. What kind of a man did that make him?

"That's bullshit, but okay. I can see you don't want to talk about it. Can I walk you back?"

Telyn sighed. "Of course. And I'm sorry. I didn't mean to cut this short." Whatever *this* was. Telyn wasn't sure what he and Lee were doing except getting to know each other, but the last few times they'd seen each other had felt almost like dates, or what Telyn imagined dates were like. He'd never been on one, so he had to make do with imagination.

"Don't worry about it. Come on, then. I'll walk you back."

Telyn had said he wanted to leave, so he couldn't go back on his words, but he made sure to walk slowly enough that he and Lee could spend more time together. He *always* wanted to spend time with Lee.

They walked side by side, closer than Telyn would have been with anyone else. He wasn't uncomfortable with Lee, though. He liked being close to him.

He was distracted from Lee when he noticed Felix and Nathan coming toward them. His stomach sank, and he looked around. He needed to hide before they could see him. Luckily for him, he and Lee were close to an alley, and he ducked into it, hoping Felix and Nathan hadn't noticed him. They'd been focused on each other, so he didn't think so.

"Telyn? What's going on?" Lee asked.

Telyn grabbed his hand and pulled him along into the alley. Lee's eyes widened, but Telyn didn't have time to explain. He peeked at the entrance of the alley and watched Felix and Nathan walk past it. They never looked his way, and he relaxed.

"Telyn? Do I need to call for help?"

Telyn shook his head. "No. I'm fine."

"I'm not sure I'd qualify hiding in an alley as fine. Who were you hiding from? Are you in danger?"

Telyn bit his lower lip. He didn't want to tell Lee what had happened with Felix and Nathan, but he knew he would eventually. They were moving toward becoming friends and maybe more, and unless he didn't want that to happen, he was going to have to open up to Lee the way Lee had done with him. The thought was scary, but it was what mates did.

"No one is after me. I just didn't want to talk to Felix and Nathan."

"Why not? They're good people. Nathan is a friend of mine."

"I know."

"You don't have to tell me, but I'll listen if you want me to."

Telyn sighed. "We should head back." This alley was nowhere near as clean as the space behind the bar, and it smelled.

Telyn tried to find a way to explain what had happened to Lee, but he knew he'd have to tell him about his mother if he wanted Lee to understand. He hated the thought. He didn't want Lee to look at him differently, but it was going to happen.

"My mother and I don't have a good relationship. She's a red demon, an ouly, and she thought I'd be one, too. But I came out pink, and only light pink at that. I've never known my father, so I don't know if he was a pink demon too. He's never been in the picture, and the few times I asked my mother about him, she freaked out. She's, well, I guess the only way to describe her is that she's abusive. She hates me. She always tells me I'm a waste of space, and she's been trying to make something out of me ever since I can remember. That's why when Felix's mother talked to her, she agreed to have us date. She thought Felix and I could get married, and since he's an ianto demon, he would have brought some prestige to our family or something like that."

Telyn swallowed. "But when I met Felix, he was already with Nathan. It was embarrassing. My mother was there, and there was yelling, and I thought Nathan would hate me for trying to steal his mate. I wasn't doing that, but it was obvious both Felix's mother and mine wanted exactly that. Both Nathan and Felix saw the way my mother treated me. Nathan was actually the one who told me to come here to Gillham if I ever needed anything."

"You didn't have anyone else who could help?"

"I don't have anyone, period—only my mother. I snuck out of the house when I decided that living on the streets would be better than living with her. She—she told me I should kill myself, and I thought about it. That was when I realized I couldn't stay."

Telyn jerked when Lee reached for him, and Lee slowed down, but he didn't stop. Telyn didn't move away when he realized what Lee was doing. Lee took his hand and tangled their fingers together in a way that shouldn't have made Telyn's heart race the way it was.

"I'm sorry you had to go through all that," Lee murmured. He pulled Telyn into the bar parking lot and looked around. "But you are *not* a waste of space, and you shouldn't listen to anything your mother said. Having a child doesn't make someone a parent. My biological parents sucked, but the people who adopted me love me as if they'd been the ones who gave birth to me. That woman isn't your mother. She's just the person who brought you into this world, and she's not part of your life anymore. She never will be, not unless you want her to."

"I don't." Telyn would be happy never to see her again. His life right now might not be perfect, but it was much better than what he'd had when he lived with her.

Lee couldn't stop thinking about what Telyn had told him at lunch. He'd tried to focus on other things—a book, then a movie—before finally deciding to make dinner. He wasn't a great cook, but even he could roast a chicken. He'd have more than enough meat for his dinner and Telyn's lunch tomorrow. He was trying to avoid always making sandwiches for his mate, even though they were the easiest thing to give him. Cold chicken would be good, though, and Telyn needed the protein.

Lee's mind was still reeling from Telyn's words. He'd known someone had been harsh to Telyn from his behavior, but he'd never imagined this. He wasn't sure why—his biological parents had been violent, both with each other and with him. He wasn't used to thinking about families that way anymore, though. He'd been adopted eleven years ago, and he'd been loved since then.

Telyn hadn't. He'd been raised by his mother, and she was one of the worst persons Lee knew of. He hadn't needed details to know that. Just the fact that she'd told her only son to kill himself was enough. When Lee thought about how close he'd come to losing Telyn before even meeting him, he wanted to throw up.

No one deserved to go through what Telyn had because of his mother. Lee wanted to give him the world because he deserved it. He deserved to be loved and cherished, and Lee was planning to do just that, for the rest of his life.

The sky rumbled outside. Lee didn't like how dark it had gotten. He'd checked the weather earlier, and the storm had been supposed to pass by Gillham without getting close. He wasn't sure that was going to be the case, though, and with Telyn out there, it made him nervous. Telyn wasn't equipped to be outside in the rain, and especially not a storm. Would he agree to come to Lee's place if Lee went out to ask him, though?

That was the big question. Now Lee understood better why Telyn didn't trust anyone, not even him. It made sense, and the pain of it had lessened, but that didn't help him find a way to convince Telyn that he didn't have to stay on the streets. Even if he didn't want to stay with Lee, he didn't have to. Kameron was more than ready to give Telyn his own apartment and help him find a job. Telyn was going to have to trust to make that happen, though.

And in the meantime, he was out there in the rain.

Lee huffed and turned off the oven. He checked the chicken, then washed his hands, grabbed his phone and his keys, and went out.

It started raining just as he walked down the street toward the bar. He should probably have taken his car, but his apartment was only five minutes away on foot from the bar. Besides, Telyn had only ever seen him walk around, so he wouldn't recognize his car. Lee didn't want to spook him by going near him in a car he didn't know.

Lee started running. He was getting soaked already, but he didn't care. He needed to get to Telyn, who was no doubt in the same state as he was and who wouldn't have a warm shower and bed waiting for him at the end of the night.

The bar parking lot was almost empty, and while it was well illuminated, Lee could barely see with the rain pounding around him and on him. Its sound was a constant that didn't allow him to hear if Telyn answered him when he called for him. "Telyn!"

Lee didn't stop moving. He rushed toward the dumpster as he continued to yell, but when he peeked behind it, the spot was empty.

Shit. This was where he'd left Telyn earlier that day, and Telyn hadn't said anything about moving somewhere else. Lee knew he liked being here because he knew Nate was safe and because he could hide easily behind the dumpster.

Where could Telyn be if he wasn't there, though?

The park was out, but maybe he was behind the shelter

where Lee had first seen him. The shelter's back door had an awning that could be useful when it rained. That was where people left animals if they couldn't abandon them at the front of the building.

The shelter wasn't far from the bar, thank God. Lee's feet splashed, water sloshing in his shoes with every step he made. He didn't even bother avoiding the puddles that were forming on the sidewalk. He was drenched, and that wasn't going to change by avoiding a puddle.

"Telyn?" Lee yelled as he got close to the shelter. He couldn't see much. Water kept dripping in his eyes no matter how many times he wiped it away.

His foot hit something, making him stumble. His foot landed in a puddle that was deeper than he'd expected. The cold water startled him, and he jerked back only to stumble on whatever had been abandoned on the sidewalk again.

Someone grabbed him before he could end up flat on his face in the water, but he was too heavy, and they both tilted forward. Lee ended up on his back while the person who'd tried to help him landed on top of him, pushing all the air out of his lungs. Lee tried to suck in a breath and to push the person away, but when his hand came into contact with long hair and a short horn, he realized *Telyn* was the person pinning him to the ground.

Telyn scrambled off Lee, but he didn't go far, kneeling next to him. "Are you okay?"

Lee nodded and sat up. He felt like he was in a pool, and he couldn't wait to go home and dry off. He never wanted to see rain again. "Are *you* okay?" he asked.

"Yes. Did something happen? You don't usually come around this late."

"I was worried about you." Lee got up and held his hand out for Telyn to take. He wasn't sure Telyn would accept it, but he did, and Lee hauled him up. "You can't stay out here, not with this storm. It's going to keep raining for a while."

Telyn stepped back. "I don't have anywhere to go."

Lee wanted to scream in frustration, but that wouldn't get him what he wanted, and he'd expected Telyn to say something like that. "You do, Telyn. Come to my apartment. You can take a shower, eat the chicken I cooked for dinner, and sleep in the guest room. I promise I won't touch you or hurt you in any way. I know you don't trust me, but I'm worried for you, and I won't be able to sleep if you stay out here. Or if you don't want to come to my place, I can call Kameron and get the keys to one of the pack's apartments. You can be alone there. That way you can be sure I won't hurt you. Just, please, don't stay out here, not with this storm."

Lee wiped the water from his face again. He wasn't sure what else he could say to convince Telyn to give this a chance. He'd been trying to do it for two weeks, and Telyn hadn't budged yet. Lee hoped that telling about his past had helped him, but he couldn't read his mind or his aura. "What about my aura?" he asked.

Telyn frowned. "What about it?"

"Can you read it to make sure I won't hurt you?"

"It doesn't work like that. It's not like feelings. Usually, the only emotions I can read are fear, grief, extreme happiness, things like that, while the rest is just an indication of how the person is."

"So you have a vague idea of who I am? You can tell I'm trustful?"

Telyn hesitated. He looked like a drowned rat, with his pink hair plastered to his face and his clothes drooping from his body, both because of the weight of the water and because Telyn was so thin. Lee desperately wanted to help him, but he didn't know how if Telyn didn't allow him to.

"You're green and blue and gold," Telyn said.

That wasn't what Lee had expected. "What?"

"Your aura. It's yellow-green, with hints of blue and gold."

"What does that mean?"

"That you love people and animals. That's you're compassionate. Truthful."

"So you believe I won't hurt you?"

Telyn nodded. "I do. I'll come to your apartment."

Telyn wasn't sure he'd made the right decision, but that didn't stop him from following Lee. He could barely see Lee in front of him with the rain pouring on his face. He had to push his hair away from his eyes repeatedly, and he wished he had a hair tie. He'd lost the last one a few days ago, though, and he hadn't bought new ones yet.

"This rain is a pain in the ass," Lee said. The sound of the rain muted his voice.

Telyn jerked when something touched his hand. He didn't completely pull away only because he realized just in time that it was Lee.

"I'm just—I don't want you to get lost, and it would be too easy with this rain."

Telyn wasn't sure what he meant, but he nodded. His cheeks flushed when Lee twined their fingers together, but he didn't have time to feel self-conscious about holding hands with a man for the first time, because Lee pulled him along as he rushed toward home.

Telyn had no idea where he was. He was trusting Lee in a way he hadn't thought he could, and he wasn't a hundred percent comfortable with it, but it was better than he'd thought. He'd taken the first step, and he hoped he'd trust Lee more easily from now on. He wanted to. He'd wanted to since that first day in the alley when Lee had been so adorably flustered at realizing Telyn was his mate—and Telyn had been terrified about the strange man sniffing him while he slept.

Lee stopped in front of a building. He pushed the glass door open and stopped in the entrance, dripping water everywhere. Telyn's backpack felt like it weighed twice the usual, logged down with water as much as Telyn felt. His clothes stuck to his skin, and he was hungry.

"Is someone going to get angry at the water?" he asked, wondering if maybe he should take his shoes off before getting into the elevator.

"Nah. I doubt we'll be the only ones walking in wet tonight."

Telyn decided to follow Lee's lead. He was the one who lived there, after all.

Telyn realized they were still holding hands only once they were in the elevator. He wasn't sure what to do about it, or if he wanted to do anything about it at all. He was confused, but it was a good kind of confused.

Then *Lee* obviously realized they were still holding hands.

Telyn could see he wasn't sure what to do about it either. At least he didn't snatch his hand away. "Is this okay?" he asked, slightly raising their linked hands.

Telyn nodded. He wasn't sure he'd even be able to get a word out, not with how flustered he felt.

Lee's beaming smile made Telyn's chest feel warm. "Good. So, I'm pretty sure you're going to want to take a shower when we get to the apartment. I don't know how your things are going to come out of your backpack, but I can lend you clothes. They'll be a bit big on you, though."

Even if the clothes in Telyn's backpack weren't wet—and he doubted that—they were dirty. He'd gone back to the bar to wash in the sink there a few times since he'd started living on the streets a few weeks ago, but it wasn't enough. He felt dirty, and he knew he probably didn't smell good. He hoped Lee couldn't smell him, but again, he doubted that, and he was ashamed of it. He didn't understand why Lee was still holding his hand. Lee knew where Telyn lived and that he didn't have access to a shower or anything. How was he not disgusted? Telyn's mother wouldn't even have let him through the door in the state he was in, yet when they left the elevator, Lee didn't hesitate to pull Telyn into his apartment.

They stopped just inside the door and looked at each other. "We should probably get rid of our clothes here," Lee said. "I mean, I won't watch or anything, but we'll get the entire apartment wet if we keep them on. I can strip and leave you here, go grab you some towels so you can shield yourself. I won't peek, but I understand you might not be comfortable with being naked with me. And once you're done showering and warming yourself up, we can eat, I cooked chicken earlier, and it should still be warm."

Telyn was overwhelmed, but for once, it was in a good way. He had no idea what he was doing or what was going to happen, but God, how he wanted Lee.

Lee had been nothing but nice to him, and he still was. He'd gone out of his way to get Telyn to a warm, dry place, and he was offering him clothes and food, and more importantly, himself. He hadn't said it out loud, but they both knew that. Telyn was Lee's mate, whether Telyn could believe it or not. And he wanted it. He might be wary and afraid to trust Lee, but he wanted him and what he could give him. He wanted to be loved and cherished the way he'd never been. He wanted to feel safe, to know he could go to sleep at night and that he didn't have to fear being woken in the middle of the night being yelled at, that no one would tell him he was eating too much or taking up too much space, or that he was useless.

Lee hadn't told him that once, even though he was homeless. He'd never looked down on him. He'd taken care of him even when he'd resisted.

And Telyn was done resisting.

He dropped his backpack to the floor. It made a squishy sound, but Telyn didn't let it bother him. Lee's eyes widened when Telyn moved toward him, hooking his hand behind Lee's neck in a move he wouldn't have dared doing even a week ago. But he did now, and he pulled Lee's head down.

Their first kiss was just a press of the lips, yet it was *so much*. Telyn had never done this, but he'd imagined it plenty of times. He gently prodded at Lee's lips with his tongue, smiling when Lee gasped and finally grabbed his waist. Lee pulled him close. Their clothes squished as they pressed against each other, and Telyn wanted them off. He was cold and wet, but he wouldn't mind it if he was cold and wet with Lee, especially if they weren't wearing clothes.

Lee's eyes went even wider when Telyn pushed away from him and peeled his t-shirt off. Telyn didn't give himself time to stop and think. If he was going to do this, he needed to push past the hesitation and awkwardness. Those weren't going anywhere, so he needed to ignore them.

"Telyn . . ." Lee started.

Telyn shook his head. He toed his shoes off, then pushed his sodden jeans and underwear down. He ignored Lee's presence because he'd freak out if he acknowledged it, and took his socks off, then threw himself back against Lee.

Lee welcomed him. He didn't try to stop things or to slow them down. Telyn trusted him to say something if he pushed too much, so he kissed Lee again.

Lee's hands stroked down Telyn's back and along his tail, skimming the top of the curve of his ass. He held Telyn close and handled him as if he were precious—smoothly, slowly, gently.

"What do you want?" Lee asked.

Telyn didn't know how to answer that. He didn't know what he wanted. "Just touch me. Please."

Lee smiled. "I can do that."

But Telyn wanted to touch Lee, too. He wanted skin instead of the wet fabric he was pressed against. He scrambled to raise Lee's t-shirt. Lee understood what he was doing, and in only a few minutes, they were both naked and plastered against each other. There was no time for Telyn to be self-conscious or to think about the consequences of what they were doing. He just wanted to *feel*.

And feel he did. Lee's hands felt like they were everywhere, skimming his skin and grabbing his flesh. He even touched Telyn's tail, which was particularly sensitive — something Telyn hadn't expected. No one had ever touched him the way Lee was doing. No one had touched him at all in too long.

But Lee was, and he seemed to know precisely where and how to touch Telyn. He was driving Telyn crazy, and Telyn didn't even care that he came fast, probably *too* fast. He panted against the skin of Lee's neck, unsure of what to do now. He wanted Lee to feel as good as he had, and the only experience he had was with himself. It couldn't be that different, could it?

He reached between them and wrapped his fingers around Lee's cock. Lee jerked and leaned closer to Telyn. Telyn took it as a sign that he was doing the right thing, so he continued. He did what he liked to do with himself, twisting his hand and thumbing the head. Lee shuddered and moaned against him, and Telyn felt powerful. He *liked* doing this to Lee. He liked being the one who was making him feel like this.

Lee clung to Telyn's shoulders so tight that Telyn feared they'd both tumble to the floor when Lee came. They didn't, but only because Telyn locked his knees as Lee cried out in his ear. He wrapped his arms around Lee and held him up, stroking his back with his tail.

Telyn wasn't sure what he liked the most — the moment of passion, or the moment after it, when they slowly came back to earth in each other's arms.

"You should go take that shower," Lee murmured. "You're cold."

Telyn felt anything but cold, but as Lee guided him to the bathroom, he couldn't help but wonder if that was it? Now that Lee had gotten what he'd wanted, was he going to ask Telyn to leave?

Telyn shouldn't have worried. When he got out of the shower, feeling clean for the first time in weeks, he found some of Lee's clothes waiting for him on the bed. Lee was in the kitchen, and his smile when he saw Telyn told Telyn more than words could have.

Lee wanted him there. He'd given him a roof over his head, clean clothes, and warm food, and more importantly, his affection and care. Even if Telyn had to leave tomorrow, he wouldn't forget this.

He never would.

CHAPTER FIVE

The apartment smelled like something had burned, and Lee wasn't surprised. Telyn had told him to relax while he took care of breakfast, so Lee had taken a shower. He clearly should have stuck with Telyn, but it was too late for that. As long as the apartment was still standing, though, everything would be fine.

"What happened?" he asked, striding into the kitchen, his hair still damp.

Telyn was standing in front of the stove and poking at something in a pan. It was a piece of charcoal, and Lee had no idea what it had been. He also didn't know how Telyn had managed to burn it that much while standing in front of it.

Telyn turned his big eyes to Lee. His tail swished behind him, sign that he was agitated. "I burned the bacon."

"That was bacon?"

Telyn's eyes narrowed. "Yes. I already turned the heat off under it."

Thank fuck for small mercies. "That's good. We should probably dump the entire pan in the sink and call it a day."

Telyn's lower lip slid out in a pout. The man shouldn't be that adorable, but he was, and Lee's heart swelled. "I wanted to cook breakfast."

"I know, but it's obvious you don't know how to do it."

Telyn looked at his feet. "I wasn't allowed in the kitchen when I lived with my mother."

With anyone else, Lee would have thought it was because they were so bad at cooking that their mother didn't want to

76

risk it, but he knew that wasn't the case for Telyn. He hadn't been allowed in the kitchen because his mother had been the one who'd controlled what he ate—or didn't eat, since she hadn't fed him close to enough. "That's okay. I'll teach you."

"You've already done so much for me. I can't ask you to do that, too."

"You're not asking. I'm offering." Lee took the fork he'd been using to poke at the charcoal from him.

They did a little sidestep, with Lee trying to get to the pan so he could throw it and its contents away while Telyn was trying to step away from the stove. Lee grinned and put a hand on Telyn's hip, using his hold to turn both of them around and take Telyn's place in front of the stove. Telyn's cheeks flushed, but he didn't move away from Lee's touch.

Things were still awkward between them, even though they'd been sharing the apartment for close to two weeks. They hadn't had sex again—which was a pity—but Telyn had been showing his affection with small touches and sometimes kisses, and that was enough for Lee. The last thing he wanted was to push Telyn.

He was terrified that Telyn would decide to go back onto the streets. He didn't want to risk Telyn's safety just because he couldn't keep his hands to himself, so he'd decided to let Telyn choose the pace. Besides, they were still getting to know each other and learning how to share a living space.

They fit together well. Telyn was trying hard to do his part of the chores, although he should probably stay away from the kitchen until he could learn how not to burn things. The fact that he'd tried was impressive, though, because he always seemed afraid to do something wrong.

Lee understood where that came from. Telyn was afraid Lee would kick him out—as if that could happen—and his mother had used everything he'd done to berate him and tell him he was a waste of space. Now he was afraid of doing something wrong, and Lee was impressed that he'd decided to give cooking a try anyway. Telyn was more relaxed, like maybe he was starting to understand that Lee didn't care about what he did wrong. He wasn't going anywhere, not unless *he* decided to go. As far as Lee was concerned, he'd be keeping his roommate for the rest of his life.

"Is there something else we can cook?" he asked, still so close to Telyn that he could feel his body heat.

Telyn licked his lips. "No. That was the last of the bacon, and we ate the eggs yesterday."

"We need to go grocery shopping, then."

Telyn took a step back. Lee dropped his hand even though it was the last thing he wanted to do. "I'm fine with whatever you choose," he murmured.

There was Telyn's mother again. "I said *we* were going to go grocery shopping, Tel. That means you and me. You live here now, so you get to choose what to eat. Even if you pick something I don't like, it doesn't mean you can't have it."

Telyn's head snapped up. Lee wasn't sure if it was at the shortening of his name or at the rest of what he'd said. "I don't want to inconvenience you."

"You're not. I need to go grocery shopping. You need to eat."

Telyn chewed on his lower lip. "Can you afford it? I don't mean to be rude, but you've been buying food and everything else for both of us, while I haven't been doing anything. It's not fair."

Lee wanted to tell him that what his mother had done to him wasn't fair, but Telyn was trying to get away from his past, and Lee didn't want to remind him of it. He knew how hard it was to leave everything behind and try to have a normal life. "I told you, the pack is paying for you right now. Kameron told me that until you felt comfortable and safe enough to find yourself a job, the pack will take care of you.

That means that he's given me enough money to buy you food and everything else you need. Don't worry about it."

"I should find a job."

As long as it wasn't anywhere near a kitchen, it probably was a good idea. Telyn had been spending the time Lee was working in the apartment, napping and catching up on everything he'd missed because of his mother. He'd watched TV, read books and magazines. It was great, but Lee suspected he was getting bored and that he was feeling the need to do *something*. Besides, finding a job would help him make friends and feel better about himself.

Telyn had so far refused to meet Lee's friends, and Lee hadn't pushed. He understood how overwhelming everything was right now. But he wanted his mate and his friends to get along, especially Brandon, who was chomping at the bit to meet Telyn.

"If that's what you want, then yes, you can get a job. Why don't we talk about it on our way to the grocery store?"

Telyn looked around the kitchen. "I should stay here and clean the mess I made."

"Or we can clean up later, together. There isn't much anyway. Come on, Telyn. You're going to have to leave the apartment if you want to get a job. This is the first step in that direction." The fact that he hadn't left yet was worrying Lee, but he tried not to obsess over it. Telyn needed to find his feet and to learn a new life. That wasn't easy, and if he felt safe in the apartment, Lee wasn't going to take that away from him.

Telyn sighed. "All right. I'll come."

Lee couldn't help but beam. "Great. That way you can help me carry the bags."

"So *that's* why you wanted me to go with you," Telyn groused, but Lee could hear the humor in his voice.

He slung one arm around Telyn's shoulders, pleased when instead of moving away, Telyn leaned against him. "Yep.

That's why I wanted you to come." Telyn wouldn't want him to worry about him, so he didn't admit to that.

Telyn was jumpy as they walked along the sidewalk after they left the apartment. He kept looking around as if he expected his mother to jump out from behind a dumpster or a car. Lee didn't say anything about it, but he moved closer, trying to communicate that even if something did happen, he'd be there for Telyn. He'd always be there for his mate, even if they never bonded.

They walked into the grocery store, and Telyn relaxed, albeit only slightly. Lee grabbed a cart and gestured: "Okay, the sky's the limit here, so grab what you want."

Telyn didn't look convinced, so Lee wasn't surprised when he didn't put anything into the cart. He kept an eye on him, though, so he managed to see when Telyn was interested in something, and once he turned the other way, Lee grabbed whatever it was and dumped it into the cart.

Telyn wouldn't like it, but he'd have to deal with it. Lee wanted to spoil his mate the way no one had until now, and he was going to do it.

Telyn wasn't blind. He'd noticed what Lee was doing almost as soon as they walked into the grocery store. That was why he wasn't looking at everything he was curious about. He didn't want Lee to buy him half the store.

He couldn't help but smile, though. Lee was adorable in the way he tried to take care of Telyn without Telyn noticing — or so he thought. But Telyn had spent too many years being aware of his mother's every movement and mood, so he didn't miss much.

They were in the middle of the cereal aisle when two men turned into it. Telyn looked up, but it was too late for him to hide unless he threw himself behind the cart, and he wasn't going to do that. It would embarrass Lee, and Telyn didn't want that.

He also didn't want to talk to Nathan and Felix, though.

"Telyn?"

Telyn closed his eyes. Of course Felix had noticed him. He was standing in the middle of the aisle, and while the marks on his skin might not be noticeable, his pink hair was. He'd wrapped his tail around his waist so it wouldn't be visible, but there was little he could do about his hair except dying it, and he didn't want to. He liked his hair. He was only now starting to be more comfortable with the fact that he was a madha demon. He didn't want to hide it.

To Telyn's surprise, Felix rushed toward him. Nathan followed him at a slower pace, but he didn't look angry. Telyn braced himself—he wasn't sure for what, but no one had ever been as happy-looking as Felix about meeting him—but Felix stopped just in front of him.

"What are you doing here? Why are you with Lee?"

Telyn blinked. He wasn't sure what to tell Felix. He didn't want to explain that after his mother had told him to kill himself, he'd left her and had lived on the streets for a few weeks before his mate had dragged him to his apartment.

"This is awkward," Nathan said as he caught up to Felix. He pushed the cart to the side so they weren't blocking the aisle and wrapped an arm around Felix's waist.

Telyn wasn't sure if it was a way for him to tell Telyn Felix was with *him*, but it wasn't like Telyn had ever wanted Felix. Felix was cute, and he seemed to be a nice man, but Telyn's heart and mind were full of Lee. He doubted that would ever change, no matter what happened between them.

"Telyn is living with me," Lee said.

Telyn blinked. He hadn't known what to tell Felix and Nathan, but he hadn't expected Lee to just come out with that.

Felix's eyes widened. "Really? What about your mother?"

"I—I moved out," he managed to say.

"Good for you. She was too similar to my mother to be a good person to live with."

Felix had no idea just how bad Telyn's mother was, and Telyn wasn't about to tell him.

"So how come you two live together?" Nathan asked.

This time, Lee looked at Telyn. They hadn't told anyone but Lee's family and his best friend that they were mates, and Telyn hadn't met them yet. He didn't want to keep it a secret, though. He knew Lee wouldn't let him go, not unless he wanted to leave, and he didn't. He *never* wanted to be away from Lee. That meant that sooner or later, people would find out about him and that they were mates, and he had to wrap his mind around that and get used to it, no matter how weird it felt.

Telyn nodded and forced himself to smile. He was so nervous his stomach churned, and he wasn't even sure why. Maybe he thought that Felix and Nathan would think he wasn't good enough for Lee. He shared that opinion, but he didn't want Lee to know about it.

Lee beamed, looking so happy it hurt Telyn's heart. "He's my mate."

Felix and Nathan both look gobsmacked, but not for long. They congratulated Lee, and to Telyn's surprise, Telyn, too. He wasn't used to people being happy for him. He wasn't used to any of this, and he wasn't sure how to react except for smiling and nodding.

"Are you two bonded yet?" Felix asked.

Telyn shook his head. "I don't know if that's a good idea."

"Well, you're both young. You have time to date and everything, although since you're already living together, it might not be long before you're ready to bond. What does your mother think about it?"

"I haven't talked to her since I left." And Telyn didn't want to see her ever again. He already knew how she'd react if he told her about Lee. She'd be surprised that Lee would debase himself that way, because who could want Telyn as a mate? Then she'd tell Telyn that obviously Lee wanted something from him, maybe his body, or maybe a servant. She'd berate Telyn for believing that he could have something real with Lee. She'd humiliate him in front of Lee.

No, Telyn never wanted to see her again.

"If you want to know what I think, you should stay away from her," Nathan intervened. "No offense, but even though I only met her once, I could tell she's an awful woman."

"You're right, she is." Telyn might feel guilty about thinking that and saying it out loud, but he'd always known it. His mother *was* an awful person, and he'd wasted too much of his life trying to hold on to their relationship and to make her happy. He knew nothing he could do would achieve that, and he was done trying.

"So what are you doing now? Except living with your mate, of course."

Telyn looked at his feet. "Nothing."

"It's been an adjustment for him," Lee intervened.

Telyn thought he should probably feel ashamed that he was letting Lee talk for him, making excuses for the fact that he was leeching off him, but he was relieved. He didn't know how to do this—make friends, talk to people as if it were normal for him. It wasn't. Telyn didn't have friends. He didn't have anyone in his life but his mother.

But not anymore. He had Lee now, and Lee came with friends and a family who wanted to meet Telyn. Telyn had managed to say no until now, but he knew he wouldn't be able to put it off forever. He didn't want to, either. He just had no idea how to behave when he'd meet them.

"It's not easy to leave your life behind," Nathan said.

"And Telyn's life wasn't great, to begin with."

Telyn didn't know Nathan's story, but from the way he looked at him, he suspected he'd been through a lot. That seemed to be a common theme with the people who lived in this town.

"It's good that he has a chance to build something better now, then."

"Are you looking for a job?" Felix asked.

Telyn hadn't been, but he knew he was going to. "Yes." He needed to start helping Lee with buying food and paying bills. No matter what Lee said, if they were going to share a life, Telyn had to be an active participator in it.

"The coffee shop is looking for people. They usually hire teenagers, but they weren't able to find everyone they needed this year. It could be a nice first job for you, tide you over until you find something you want to do. Or would you rather go back to school?"

Telyn shook his head. He wasn't going to tell Felix he'd never been to school. "The coffee shop sounds good." It sounded *terrifying*, but Telyn was going to have to get over that fear and put himself out there.

Felix gently smiled, as if he could see how scared Telyn was. "Jessie and his brother own the shop. They're good people, and pack members. I don't know if you've already talked to Kameron, but since you're Lee's mate, you're basically family. That means something to the pack. It's going to take some time to get used to it, but you're not alone anymore."

"You sound like you know what you're talking about," Telyn murmured.

"I do. I cut the ties with my mother, too. I don't want her in my life when she can't accept Nathan is here to stay. You're not alone, though, Telyn. It's strange and sudden, but you have an entire pack behind you now, and of course, Lee."

Telyn had known that, but hearing it from someone he barely knew was different. He had a family. He had Lee.

And he needed to be good enough for both of them.

Lee hadn't been sure what would happen when Felix and Nathan had appeared in front of them, but he was glad they had. Telyn had been uncomfortable, especially in the beginning, but he wasn't living on the streets anymore, and there was nothing shameful in living with his mate. Not that there had been anything shameful about his situation before he'd agreed to move in with Lee, but Lee knew that was how Telyn saw things.

After the years during which his mother had told him time and time again that he wasn't good enough, he'd felt that way, and he still did. It was going to take a little while for him to really believe he was good enough to do anything he wanted—and that he was more than good enough for Lee. Lee wouldn't trade him for anyone else.

"We should see each other sometime," Felix said. "Maybe at the coffee shop? That way Telyn can see it'll be a piece of cake for him to work there."

"That's a good idea. Give me your number," Lee said. He understood that Felix was trying to be friendly, but he could see Telyn was overwhelmed.

They needed to finish their grocery run and go home so Telyn could relax and have some quiet time before he had to make a decision about where he'd work, or even if that was something he wanted to do. Lee knew Telyn felt he had to, even though it wasn't necessary. Kameron would make sure Telyn and Lee had enough money to have a good life until Telyn found something he *wanted* to do. Kameron wanted his pack members to be happy. That meant that he didn't push them into taking jobs they might not want just because they didn't have another option, especially when it came to people whose life had been hell before they'd arrived in Gillham, people who hadn't had a chance to live their life the way they wanted.

Telyn relaxed once Felix and Nathan left. Lee left him alone, picking stuff from the shelves at random.

"You don't like tuna," Telyn said.

Lee blinked at his hand. Sure enough, he'd been dumping canned tuna into his cart. "Maybe you do."

"Maybe, but I'm not going to make you cook it for me since you don't like it." Telyn took the can from Lee's hand and put it back onto the shelf. "We should finish shopping and go home. I'm hungry."

Lee grinned. Telyn so seldomly asked for things that he wanted to present him with a meal right now. "We can take the groceries up to the apartment and go to the coffee shop to grab something to eat."

Telyn eyed the cart. "Or we could cook some of the things we're buying."

"We're already buying it and taking it home. We can cook it later."

They managed to get through the rest of the shopping without Telyn putting anything back on the shelves. Lee smiled when he noticed his mate sneak some chocolate into the cart. He'd buy him all the chocolate he could ever want, but he knew this was a big step for Telyn. He'd picked something he wanted—not that he needed but wanted—without asking Lee if he could. Lee also hadn't needed to gently push him to do it.

They were in the parking lot, laden with bags, when Telyn froze. Like always when his mate had that kind of reaction, Lee looked around, ready to defend Telyn from whatever was scaring him. He didn't see anything, though, or at least, nothing that could be interpreted as a threat. There were a few people walking to and from the store, some hanging around their car loading them, and a big guy leaning against a tree at the back of the parking lot.

"Telyn? What's wrong?" Lee asked. Even though he couldn't identify the threat, it didn't mean there wasn't one. Maybe one of the women was Telyn's mother. They all looked human, but maybe they were hiding their demon particularities. Telyn's marks were barely visible, so maybe the same went for his mother.

But Telyn wasn't looking at any of the women. He was staring at the big guy against the tree instead.

"Do you know him?" Lee asked. He ignored the spike of jealousy in his guts and focused on Telyn.

Telyn shook his head and took a step back. "No."

"You can tell me whatever happened, Telyn. I promise I won't judge."

"It's not that. I don't know him, but I've seen him around." Telyn licked his lips. "I think he's a drug dealer."

Lee wasn't surprised. The number of dealers in town had gone up ever since the Beasts had decided to get revenge on Kameron for something or other. It looked like they were trying to kill as many shifters as possible with their drugs, and they'd succeeded, up to a point. Several people had died, and Lee and Brandon had lost Nathalie. Kameron and the police force in Gillham were trying to get their hands on the people responsible for the dealing, but the Beasts were slippery, and even when they did manage to arrest some of them, more Beasts popped up. It was like a never-ending whack-a-mole game, but with bloodthirsty assholes.

"How do you know?" Lee asked.

"I saw him a few times. He gave something in a small bag to another man, who gave him money for it. I don't know for sure that it was drugs, but what else could it be?"

"You're right. Have you told anyone about it?"

Telyn shook his head. His pink hair slid in front of his face, and he hid behind it, careful not to look at the dealer again.

"No. I didn't know who to tell."

"Okay, how about this — we go home to put the groceries away. I'll call one of our pack members in the meantime. He's a detective, and he's been trying to stop the Beasts since they got into town. He hasn't managed yet because they're slippery as fuck, so he'll be happy to hear about this."

"I didn't know if I could help."

"You just have to tell him what you saw."

Telyn bit his lower lip. "What about the time I spent living on the streets?"

"What about it? I'd suggest you be honest with Patrick. He won't care. But if you'd rather avoid telling him about that, you can tell him you've been living with me ever since you arrived in Gillham. He's mated, so he'll understand that we rushed into things." Lee took one of Telyn's hands. He had to put down the bags he was holding, and he hoped the ice cream wasn't going to melt while he tried to reassure Telyn, but that was secondary. "You'll be okay, Telyn. You're my mate. That means no one can take you away from me. If they try, they'll have to answer to the council."

"You think I could help people by talking to your friend?"

"I do. Like I said, no matter how hard Patrick is working, he's having trouble identifying the dealers. When he does, new ones arrive."

"So it wouldn't be much. Even if he arrests this man, new ones will come."

"Probably, but in the meantime, there will be one less dealer on the streets, and if we're lucky, the guy might be higher up on the food chain and know something we can use to stop the Beasts."

Lee could see Telyn wasn't convinced, and he wouldn't force him to talk to Patrick if he didn't want to. He'd rather go himself and explain what he knew, even though it would mean Patrick would have questions he couldn't answer.

Telyn sighed. "All right. I'll talk to him. Will you stay with me when I do?"

"Of course." And Lee would ask Patrick if they could meet outside of the police station, maybe at the coffee shop for lunch. That way Telyn wouldn't be as intimidated as he clearly was already. "I'm not going anywhere until you tell me you don't want me by your side anymore, Telyn. I thought you knew that."

Telyn smiled. "I do. It's nice to hear it, though."

Lee should have realized that. Telyn had only heard how much his mother hated him all his life. He needed to be told he was loved and cherished now, and that his life mattered.

Because it did. Lee needed Telyn to be happy, even if it wasn't with him. He hoped Telyn would fall in love with him eventually, though, just like he was falling in love with Telyn.

The day had started out so well, but Telyn hated how it had crashed down. It wasn't even meeting Felix and Nathan at the grocery store that had been the worst part, even though Telyn had been anything but comfortable when it had happened. No, the worst part had been seeing that drug dealer in the parking lot and having to talk to the police about it.

Telyn had been jumpy ever since then. He knew the detective he'd talked to wouldn't call his mother. Patrick didn't have a reason to, not when Telyn was twenty-two and had left his house voluntarily. Telyn had skipped telling him about living on the streets like Lee had suggested, because seeing the drug dealer had nothing to do with that, but he thought Patrick suspected he'd kept some things to himself. He supposed he was lucky the man hadn't pushed for more answers than he was ready to give.

"Tired?" Lee asked as they walked back home.

Telyn nodded. He hadn't done anything all day except for

grocery shopping and talking to Patrick, yet he felt like he could sleep a week. He hated how the day had gone and that he and Lee hadn't had time to be together, although that wasn't just because of what had happened.

They'd been dancing around each other since the night of the storm. Lee wasn't pushing or demanding anything from Telyn, even though he was letting Telyn live with him. He hadn't asked for money or sex or anything else. It had surprised Telyn in the beginning, but now that he was getting to know Lee, he realized it shouldn't have.

It left him feeling hesitant, though. Things would have been easier if Lee had wanted things from him, but he didn't, and if *Telyn* wanted something, he was going to have to ask for it or take the first step. The problem was that Telyn had no idea how to do that. He knew Lee was nothing like his mother, but the thought of exposing himself, of telling Lee what he felt and wanted, was terrifying.

Lee wrapped an arm around Telyn's shoulders. He paused, no doubt waiting to see if Telyn was going to move away, but instead, Telyn snuggled closer to Lee. They hadn't been overly affectionate when they were together, but that didn't mean Telyn didn't want it. He just didn't know how to initiate it or ask for it. Having Lee take the first step like he just had was easy, and Telyn could let himself enjoy the hug.

"How about we have ice cream when we get home?" Lee suggested.

"I don't know. I'm not hungry."

"That's because you don't eat when you're stressed. It's not good for you, though. I mean, I love you and the way you look, but you're so thin, Tel."

Telyn froze in the middle of the sidewalk. His legs refused to take one more step because his brain was stuck on what Lee had just said.

Lee loved him?

Telyn realized it shouldn't be that much of a surprise. Lee was letting him live with him. He took care of him. He was always there when Telyn needed something, and he made sure Telyn didn't push himself too much while at the same time gently pulling him into doing things he had to do. Telyn was also Lee's mate, so it wasn't surprising that Lee felt those three little words.

But no one had ever told Telyn they loved him. He was pretty sure no one *had* loved him before. His mother certainly didn't, and he'd never known his father. He didn't have friends. He didn't have anyone.

But now, he did.

Lee faced Telyn, a frown on his face. "Tel? Are you okay? What's wrong? Did you see that guy again? I can call Patrick and ask him to come."

Telyn shook his head. Even the fact that Lee called him *Tel* made him realize there was so much more between them than he'd let himself think about until now.

"What is it, then?" Lee asked. He took one of Telyn's hands in his and pulled him closer to the flower shop they'd stopped in front of so people would be able to pass by them on the sidewalk. "Are you okay?"

"I am." Telyn licked his lips. What if Lee hadn't meant what he'd said? Maybe it had just slipped out. Maybe he was just used to reassuring his friends and his family by telling them he loved them. The only way Telyn could be sure of it was to ask, and he didn't know if he was strong enough to take a denial.

"Tel, you're freaking me out," Lee said. His voice was urgent, and it told Telyn just how worried he was.

Telyn didn't think that even if he hadn't meant it, Lee would be cruel about this. It wouldn't be him, and Telyn thought he knew him enough after they'd spent the past few weeks together. Lee was a good man, albeit a bit impulsive when it came to the people he loved. He was also a bit pushy, but he knew when to stop. He'd showed that enough with Telyn.

"What you said," Telyn started, but he wasn't sure how to finish that sentence.

"When?"

"Just now." Telyn closed his eyes. "You said you love me." And the way he looked, but that wasn't what Telyn's brain and heart had latched on.

"Oh."

Telyn didn't dare open his eyes, not when he didn't know how to read Lee's expression and voice. That *oh* hadn't sounded good, though, had it?

A hand cupped Telyn's cheek. "Tel, of course I meant it. I wish I hadn't blurted it out in the middle of the street like an idiot, but where and how I told you doesn't change the way I feel. I love you, Telyn."

Telyn didn't know what to say. He knew he should tell Lee he loved him too, and he did, but the words couldn't seem to pass his lips. He swallowed and tried again, opening his eyes to find Lee looking at him. How could he have missed that Lee loved him when it was right there in his eyes?

Lee smiled softly. "You don't have to say it back. I know you love me too."

Telyn laughed. He suddenly felt lighter, lighter than he ought to be after the day they'd had. "You sound convinced of that."

"I am. You're my mate. You have to love me. And before you even think about it, I'm joking. I really should learn to watch what I say to you. I don't love you because you're my mate. I love you because you're brave and sexy and so strong. Every time you're in the room, I can't look away from you, and when we're not together, I miss you like crazy. The fact that we're mates is just a bonus because it means that I'll never lose you."

Telyn nodded. "I don't want to lose you."

"You're not going to. I'm not going anywhere, Telyn. I promise. I'll stay with you through everything you'll have to face, be it your mother or that drug dealer."

"Because you love me."

Lee grinned. "Because I love you."

Telyn didn't think he'd ever felt this way. He was warm and happy, almost giddy. Was this what love felt like? Because if it was, he knew he never wanted to stop loving Lee.

Lee gently kissed Telyn. "I know things are weird and hard right now. You're still not settled into this new life of yours, and that's okay. It's going to take time, and we should probably talk about what's coming next, both for you and for the two of us as a couple. But I need you to know that I'm not going anywhere. I intend to be in your life for as long as you let me."

Telyn wrapped his fingers around Lee's wrist. "It's going to be for a very long time, then."

Lee's answering smile was the most gorgeous thing Telyn had ever seen. "That's what I was aiming for. And I know things aren't easy for you right now. I know you're still not sure you can trust me."

Telyn opened his mouth to say he did trust Lee, but Lee shook his head and continued, "It's okay if you don't, Tel. we've only known each other a month. But I'm going to do everything I can to show you we belong together, and that we can have a happy future. I just need you to tell me if I push too hard, or if you're not comfortable with something. I can't know if you don't tell me."

"As long as *you* tell *me* if I'm doing something wrong."

"Deal."

Telyn was still afraid of what the future would bring him, but now that he knew Lee would be by his side when he faced it, he knew things would be okay.

Chapter Six

L ee could tell Telyn was nervous. His tail was twitching behind him as he got ready to go to work for the first time, and while he was doing his best to appear relaxed, Lee wasn't fooled. He'd learned to read his mate's behavior and his reactions, but even if he hadn't, he'd have known. Who wasn't nervous on their first day of work? Lee had been, and he didn't have the baggage Telyn did.

"You'll be perfect," he said even though he knew Telyn wouldn't believe him. He'd been put down too many times by his mother, and it would take him a while to get used to compliments and to accept them.

Telyn's cheeks flushed. "I don't know." He looked at his reflection again. He was wearing a t-shirt with the logo of the coffee shop and a pair of jeans, and Lee thought he was both adorable and hot as hell.

He got up from the bed and slid behind Telyn. He wrapped his arms around Telyn's waist and kissed his neck, smiling when Telyn shivered. "You'll be great. You got this, Tel. And if you don't, Jessie and Max won't care. You're new at this. They'll help you, and even if you drop stuff or whatever, no one will berate you for that."

Lee could tell his words weren't getting through, but then, he hadn't expected them to. The only thing that would make Telyn feel better was to go to work and see he could do it. "I'll walk with you to the coffee shop, okay?"

Telyn turned and hugged Lee back. "You don't need to do that. I can do this on my own."

"I know you can. It doesn't mean you have to, though. I told you I'd be there for you, whatever you need. That includes you needing some support on your first day at work."

Lee hated Telyn's mother. He'd never met her, but he'd seen the damage she'd done to Telyn ever since they'd met. He had to live with that damage and to try somehow to help Telyn heal it, but he had no idea how to do that. Telyn was doing a good job on his own already, but Lee wanted to do more. He wasn't going to solve this right now, though.

Telyn was on the right path to healing his life, and he was doing it mostly on his own. He had a job. He shared an apartment with Lee. He was tentative friends with Nathan and Felix. He'd left his old life and his mother behind, and that had been the biggest step to take. The rest would come on its own.

Telyn wrapped his tail around his waist before they left. He didn't hide it under his t-shirt like he usually did, maybe because the t-shirt he'd been given was too tight. It was good to see him not trying to hide, though. Demons weren't a common sight in town, but Noah and Demi came around often enough that people had stopped staring at them—and at Telyn. Lee loved Telyn's tail, and the rest of him, but he understood it made Telyn self-conscious.

They walked hand in hand, and Lee stood straight. He was proud to be seen with Telyn, and he wanted Telyn to know that. He could feel that Telyn was more hesitant even though they weren't bonded, but he didn't take his hand away, and that was good enough for Lee.

"What if I mess things up?" Telyn suddenly asked.

"Then you try again."

"You make it sound so easy."

"That's because it is. No one was born knowing how to do everything, including how to make coffee or whatever your duties will be. Everyone has to learn, and in the beginning, you probably *will* make mistakes. But you'll learn, and no one will berate you for not managing to make a soy milk caramel espresso or whatever on the first try. And if you're worried, you can use me as a guinea pig for as long as you want. I'll drink everything you make and honestly tell you what I think about it."

Telyn's smile made Lee's heart flutter. "Thank you."

"You can always count on me, Tel. You need to remember that. Whatever happens, if you lose your job, or if your mother finds you, or if you decide you don't want to bond with me, it won't change anything. I'll still be there for you. Even if we break up—"

"I don't want to break up with you."

Lee grinned. "Good, because I don't want that either. And I don't want us to rush into anything. We're still kids, and you haven't had a nice start in life. We can take all the time we need to get to know each other and to decide what we want from our future." Because Telyn might not know what he wanted to do in his life, but neither did Lee. He liked working at the shelter, but he didn't know if he wanted to make a career out of it or if he'd rather go to college. Now he had Telyn to think about as well as himself, and he didn't want to leave Gillham, not when Telyn was just starting to settle here.

They stopped in front of the coffee shop, and Telyn took a deep breath. Lee wished he could do this for him, but he also knew that Telyn needed to do this on his own and that he was ready for it. He'd spent more than enough time isolating himself in the apartment. It was time for him to step into the world and see what it had to offer him. In this case, it was a job and hopefully, new friends.

Telyn let go of Lee's hand and opened the door. The coffee-scented air smelled delicious, but Lee stayed back. He needed to let Telyn do this on his own, and that meant keeping some distance. He would have gone home, but he noticed Kameron and Patrick sitting at a table in the back, their heads close as they talked. Kameron hadn't yet met Telyn, so he'd probably be curious. Lee didn't want to interrupt them, but he should warn Kameron at the very least. Telyn might freak out if the alpha tried talking to him today, of all days.

Lee peeked at Telyn before heading toward the table, but he was focused on Jessie and whatever he was saying. He had a little frown on his face, but he was nodding, and he didn't look worried.

Lee waved at Kameron when he raised his head and noticed him. Kameron smiled, and when Lee got to the table he shared with Patrick, he snatched the alpha's drink and sniffed at it. "Black?"

Kameron grinned. "Like my soul."

"Please. Everyone knows you're a softie. Can I sit with you guys? It's Telyn's first day, and I hope having me hanging around will help keep him calm." Lee sipped at Kameron's coffee and grimaced. He wasn't a flavored coffee fan, but he did need some sugar in it.

"We were just talking about the man your mate told us about," Patrick said, gesturing at one of the empty chairs at the table.

Lee flopped down and pushed Kameron's coffee back toward him. "Did you find him yet?"

"No." Patrick sounded frustrated. "You'd think it would be easy, since Telyn even gave us a description of the man's tattoos, but it's like the guy's a ghost. No one has seen him, and I'm not even sure where to start looking for him."

"How hasn't anyone seen him? I mean, I was with Telyn at the grocery store last week, and the dealer is huge."

Patrick rubbed his forehead. "I don't know what to tell you. It's possible the guy spends most of his time in his animal form in the woods. It's something we're exploring. And since I'm sure he's a Beast member, I'm going through the known members to try to identify him, but it's slow going."

"Damn. You don't think he's going to come after Telyn, do you?"

"Nah. I haven't told anyone about Telyn. It's not like I have a lot to go on right now anyway."

Lee relaxed. He knew life could be dangerous even without having the Beasts after you, but he'd seen what had happened with Brandon, and he didn't want Telyn to be in danger."

"It's your mate's first day?" Kameron asked.

Lee couldn't help but look at Telyn. He was still listening to Jessie, who was showing him how to work the espresso machine. "Yeah. He was a bit nervous, so I decided to come along."

"How is he settling?"

"It's slow going, but it's going. That's the important part." Telyn was putting down roots in Gillham, and Lee's were already there.

Telyn listened to what Jessie was telling him. He needed to get this right. He *had* to, even though he knew Jessie wouldn't kick him out if he didn't. That was the first thing Jessie had told him when he'd arrived.

You're allowed to make mistakes, and we'll work together to correct them.

It was strange to think that way. Telyn's mother had always asked a lot from him, perfection even. Of course, it had been too much for Telyn, and she'd taken pleasure in pointing out everything he did wrong and yelling at him for being an idiot. Jessie wouldn't do that, though. He'd been nothing but helpful and reassuring since Telyn had walked in, and Telyn was starting to relax.

"Why don't you try taking the next order?" Jessie said.

Anxiousness rose in Telyn again. "Are you sure? It's probably best if I just watch you for a while longer."

Jessie smiled and patted Telyn's hand. "Maybe, but you'll

learn faster if you do it. Besides, Kameron takes his coffee black. You can't get an easier order than that."

Telyn blinked at the big man on the other side of the counter. He recognized the name, of course, and he wasn't quite sure how to behave. "Alpha Rhett," he said, hoping it was the right way to address the man.

"Call me Kameron. And don't worry about coming around to meet me. Lee told me about your past, and I don't want you to push yourself too hard. There will be time for us to talk once you've settled down in your life."

Telyn felt a bit better and forced himself to smile. "What can I get you, then?"

"A black coffee, just like Jessie said. Make it the biggest one you have. I'll need it to continue working."

Jessie tsked. "Zach isn't going to be happy."

"Zach won't find out about it."

Telyn had to smile at the teasing. He doubted most of the alphas would let one of their people talk to them like Jessie was, but Kameron Rhett seemed to be a good man, at least from what Telyn knew about him. It was a relief not to have to fear he'd be kicked out if he did something wrong.

He managed to get Kameron's coffee ready without spilling everything and needing Jessie's help only once. Jessie took care of ringing up the alpha's purchase, and Telyn allowed himself to relax. He could do this. He *was* doing this. It was the first time he'd had a job, and while he knew everything wasn't always going to be as smooth as it was going now, he was starting to believe nothing bad would happen to him even if he did make a mess.

That was when his mother walked into the coffee shop.

Telyn was cleaning the counter and smiling at Jessie singing along with the music. He knew Lee was still somewhere in the shop, but when he looked up to see where he was, his gaze stopped on his mother.

Telyn dropped the mugs he'd just picked up. They clanged onto the counter, and one of them dropped to the floor, shattering. Everyone turned to look at him, but he couldn't look away from his mother. She'd turned, too, and their gazes had locked. Telyn didn't know what she was thinking, but he could tell it wasn't pleasant from the way her lips twisted.

She made a beeline for him. He'd expected it, but he still couldn't move. How had she found him? She didn't usually come to Gillham, although he might be wrong about that. He wasn't often allowed to go out with her. Maybe she came to Gillham often, and he just hadn't known about it. He should have picked a town further away from their home, but he hadn't, and now he was there, and she was there, and she looked like she was going to kill him.

"What are you doing here, Telyn? Are you working? Who on earth would give you a job where you can burn things? How did you convince them? Do you know what you've put me through, leaving the house like you did, not telling me where you were going? And don't think I haven't noticed that you stole money from me. Maybe it's a good thing you found a job, because I expect you to give it all back, along with interest. You'll have to keep your job to manage that, and I'm not sure you'll manage."

Telyn swallowed. He wanted to tell her to leave him alone. He'd thought about this moment ever since he'd left home, and he'd rehearsed what he might say.

So of course, he couldn't even get a word out.

"You have to leave your job as soon as you earned enough. I found another match for you, and I don't want your future husband to know you're working in this place." Her tone on the last word told Telyn—and everyone else in the coffee shop—what his mother thought about the shop.

Something twisted in Telyn's stomach. He'd learned to deal with his mother and her rudeness, but Jessie and Max hadn't earned it. They'd welcomed him and had given him a job even though he'd told them he didn't know how to do anything.

"You're rude, lady."

Telyn's eyes widened. He'd expected Lee to intervene, or maybe Kameron or Jessie, but instead, Felix and Nathan were standing behind his mother, and Felix looked furious. He probably remembered Telyn's mother from the last time they'd met, and he didn't look happy to see her again.

Telyn's mother turned to face Felix. Her eyes narrowed. "It's you."

Felix put his hands on his hips. His aura was violet and white, but also muted red—he was angry. "Yes, it's me, and like I said, you're rude. You need to leave if you don't have anything nice to say."

"How dare you, young man? The fact that you and my son were engaged—"

Nathan snorted loudly. "Engaged? Please. You dragged your son here and tried to get Felix to marry him, and you pitched a fit when Felix told you to fuck off because he'd met his mate."

Telyn cringed. His mother wouldn't care about the language Nathan had used. She could swear with the best of them. But she was going to unleash her anger on Nathan and Felix, and that was never a good thing.

She opened her mouth, no doubt to yell at Nathan, but Kameron stepped in. "I'm sorry, is there something wrong?" he asked. His voice was calm and steady, something Telyn wished he was. His mother always agitated him, even though she didn't have a say in his life anymore.

She looked at Kameron. "You interrupted me."

Kameron crossed his arms over his chest and arched a brow. "Yes, I did, because you were rude. You have no place here. You should leave."

"Not without my son."

"I doubt your son is happy to see you, from what I know about you."

That brought her attention back to Telyn. He resisted the urge to hide under the counter, but it was a near thing. "Telyn? What is this man saying? Did your good-for-nothing ass slander me?"

Telyn couldn't do this. He couldn't face her. He wished he could, that he were strong enough, but he wasn't. He'd come into work today, hoping it would go well, but he didn't think he'd be able to come back, so who cared if he left?

He shook his head and backed down. His back hit something, and it fell. He used that moment to sneak from behind the counter and went to the door. He heard people calling after him — *Lee* calling after him along with the others — but he ignored everyone and left the coffee shop.

His life was ruined. Everything he'd worked so hard to obtain over the past month was gone, broken by his mother. He wasn't surprised, but he wanted to kill her, to yell at her that she was a terrible mother that shouldn't have been allowed to have a child.

He didn't know where to go, what to do, but his feet took him home to Lee's apartment. Telyn didn't think Lee would kick him out, but he knew he wouldn't be able to show his face around town, not after what his mother had done, and not with the way she'd treated him.

He was ashamed. He'd always known he wasn't strong, and now everyone else knew it, too.

Lee didn't wait to see what would happen to Telyn's mother. He didn't care, and with Kameron and Patrick there, he knew she was in good hands. He rushed out, not saying goodbye to anyone, and went after Telyn.

Telyn was fast, though. The time it had taken Lee to decide to go after him had been enough for him to disappear from the sidewalk. Not being able to see him made Lee nervous. Where was he? Where would he go in the state of mind he was in? Lee hoped he'd go home, but they hadn't been together long, and he wasn't sure Telyn considered his apartment home yet. There was only one way to find out.

Lee ran along the sidewalk, apologizing to the people he bumped into but never slowing down. He managed to peek into the alleys he ran by as he did so, just in case Telyn was hiding in one of them, but by the time he got to their apartment building, he hadn't found his mate yet. Telyn had his keys with him, though, and Lee hoped he was home right now. He didn't know where he'd look for him if he wasn't, but he was ready to call Kameron and have half the pack help him.

"Telyn?" he called out as soon as he managed to get the apartment door open. It wasn't locked, and he was sure he'd locked it when they'd left earlier.

Telyn didn't answer, though. Lee closed the door behind himself and looked around. The tiny entrance was empty, as was the kitchen. He looked in the living room, but there was no one there, and he prayed he'd find Telyn in the bedroom.

He did.

Lee breathed easier when he saw the pink hair peeking from beside the bed. It looked like Telyn was hiding in the space between the bed and the wall. Lee carefully moved closer. He didn't want to startle his mate or to scare him. "Telyn?"

When Telyn still didn't answer, Lee got worried. Telyn's mother hadn't touched him from what Lee had seen, but that didn't mean that she hadn't gotten through to him. He was so fragile when it came to her and his self-worth, and now that Lee had met his mother, he understood why. The woman was a witch, and that was an insult for witches. He hoped Kameron had kicked her out of town, but he wouldn't mind doing it himself if he had the chance.

Lee knelt in front of Telyn. Telyn was curled into a tight ball, his arms wrapped around his legs, his face hidden between his knees. His hair had fanned around his face, hiding it completely. His tail was on the floor, not moving, not even when Lee gently touched it.

"Tel? Come on, talk to me," Lee crooned. He was starting to freak out, because he hadn't gotten a reaction yet, and it wasn't normal. Even if he wanted to be alone, Telyn would have told him. Instead, he wasn't even moving. It was like he wasn't aware Lee was there with him, and nothing Lee was saying was getting through to him.

Lee leaned back. What could he do? Should he call Kameron and ask him for help? He wanted to, but he knew Telyn would hate that. After what had happened at the coffee shop, Telyn wanted to hide, and Lee got it. He needed to understand that Lee was the one person he never had to hide from, though. Lee didn't care what his mother had said or how rude she'd been.

He needed to do something. Telyn wasn't reacting to his human form, but maybe he would react to his solenodon one. Talking to an animal was different than talking to a person, even though Telyn would know it was still Lee.

Lee reached out and gently stroked Telyn's hair. "Okay, love. I'm about to strip and shift. Please, try talking to me once I'm in my solenodon form. It'll make things easier for you, and you need to get whatever's wrong out. I won't judge you, and I'm not going anywhere. I love you. No amount of yelling from your mother is going to change that." He wanted to pull Telyn into his arms, but he didn't think Telyn was ready for that, so he moved away.

Lee made quick work of getting rid of his clothes and

shifting. It was always a shock for him to end up in a smaller form—he really should shift more often—but he shifted as fast as he could because he needed to focus on Telyn, who still hadn't moved. Now that he was in his animal form, Lee could smell the tears, and his heart ached for Telyn.

He touched Telyn's leg with his nose, and when Telyn still didn't react, Lee decided to force his way in. Telyn needed to get out of whatever reaction he was having. He was letting his mother influence his life, and she had no right to it and his happiness.

Lee pushed his head into the space between Telyn's arm and his thigh. There wasn't much, but Lee was small and determined. The fact that Telyn finally seemed to realize that something was happening helped, because he looked up, freeing some more space for Lee.

Lee settled his body in the groove between Telyn's chest and his thigh and rose on his back feet, pressing his front feet against Telyn's chest. Their noses almost touched, and Lee was relieved when Telyn chuckled and stroked a finger on top of his head.

He knew what Telyn was seeing. Lee was tiny in his solenodon form, with a dark brown coat of fur and a long nose, which he wiggled to get a laugh out of his mate. It worked, although Lee wished Telyn's laughter was stronger.

"What are you doing?" Telyn asked in a murmur.

Lee couldn't answer him, so he stuck his nose against Telyn's neck. That finally made Telyn laugh harder, and it was almost the same as when he was happy.

"I get it. You want to talk."

Lee nodded. He turned onto himself a few times, then settled in a ball in Telyn's lap. Telyn carefully extended his legs to give Lee more space. He closed his eyes and leaned the back of his head against the wall, but he didn't stop stroking Lee's fur.

"I hate that you and everyone else in the coffee shop had to see what happened," Telyn finally said. He groaned. "God, even the *alpha* was there, and Patrick, and Jessie. How am I supposed to show my face around town again?"

Lee bumped his head against Telyn's hand in what he hoped Telyn would recognize as a gentle scolding. He wanted to tell Telyn that no one would care about what had happened because what his mother had done didn't reflect on him, but he didn't want to risk Telyn closing off again. He'd been so scared when Telyn hadn't answered earlier, and he didn't want to go through that again.

"You know, it would be easier to talk if you were human," Telyn pointed out, but he didn't stop burying his fingers into Lee's fur, so Lee had no intention of shifting, not for a bit. Besides, it felt good to be petted. He *really* needed to shift more often. Maybe now that he and Telyn were settling down, he could. He'd take Telyn to pack territory, introduce him to his parents and to Brandon, then shift and play with him in the forest. And Telyn might want to meet Noah and Demi, too. They could understand him better than Lee could in some ways, and maybe having other demons as friends would help him see he belonged in Gillham.

Of course, getting rid of his mother might help, too, but Lee wasn't about to go out to do that. He trusted Kameron to do what needed to be done and make it clear to the horrible woman that she wasn't welcome in Gillham.

"I'm not going to lose you, am I?" Telyn asked. There was wonder in his voice, as if he hadn't expected Lee to still want him after what had happened at the coffee shop.

Lee rolled his eyes, and that earned him another chuckle from Telyn.

"You're cute like this, but I think I prefer your human form. I like it when you hug me," Telyn said, his cheeks flushed.

Lee grinned and shifted, right there in Telyn's lap.

Telyn knew he was blushing—how could he not, with Lee sitting on top of him completely naked? "What are you doing?"

Lee grinned. He seemed completely at ease, and knowing him, he probably was. "You said it would be easier for me to hug you if I were in my human form."

"That didn't mean you had to shift."

"You want me to shift back?"

"No." Telyn's hands were trembling, but he reached out and dragged Lee closer. He buried his face against Lee's throat and breathed in and out. He wasn't a shifter, but Lee's scent was calming, and that was what Telyn needed right now.

Lee stopped teasing and hugged Telyn back. He rubbed his nose against Telyn's neck, and Telyn suspected he was thinking about how his mark would be there when they bonded. Telyn wanted to do it now, but he knew it was for the wrong reason. He didn't want to bond with Lee just to make sure Lee wouldn't leave him after what had happened or because he thought Telyn was weak. Even though he suspected Lee would say yes if he asked him to bond, neither of them was in the right state of mind, and that was okay. Telyn needed to believe in himself and that he was worthy of love before taking that step.

"Do you want to go back to the coffee shop?" Lee asked.

Telyn didn't have to think about it. "Not today. Do you think I can really go back tomorrow?"

"Yeah. We can call Jessie to make sure if you want, but I'm ready to bet he'll be the first one to tell you to take the day off."

Telyn cleared his throat. "You need to get off me so I can call."

Lee leaned back, but he stayed right where he was. "Do

you want me to call?"

"No." Telyn did want Lee to call, but he knew it was something *he* had to do.

"I'll just get dressed, then."

Telyn wanted to say no. He wanted to take advantage of this moment and lose himself in Lee's body, but it wasn't the right time. People were probably worried about him and where he'd gone, and he owed it to them to reassure them.

Lee leaned forward again and gently kissed Telyn. "We'll have time for whatever you were thinking about later, but we should go grab some lunch after you call Jessie."

Telyn never wanted to leave the apartment again, but Lee was right. He couldn't hide out like he'd done the first two weeks he'd been there. Going out for lunch would put fewer expectations on him than waiting until he had to go to work tomorrow. If he felt like running today, he could. If it happened tomorrow, he'd have to deal with it and stay where he was.

Jessie was reassuring when Telyn finally called him to apologize. He cursed Telyn's mother a few times, making Telyn smile and relax. Lee was right—no one seemed to hold what had happened against Telyn, but rather, against his mother.

"Where do you want to eat?" Lee asked once Telyn put down the phone.

"Here?" Telyn asked, even though he already knew that wasn't going to happen.

Lee wrinkled his nose. "I suppose we can look to see what we have in the fridge."

He really was ready to do just about anything for Telyn, wasn't he?

Telyn sighed. "We should go out. Maybe see if Nate has already opened the bar? I'd rather not go back to the coffee shop today."

"I don't know. It's probably a bit early to go to the bar."

"I won't drink." Telyn had never touched alcohol, and he wasn't going to start now. He wasn't up for anything new right now.

Lee rolled his eyes. "I know that. Let's hope Nate is open, then. He's been opening for lunch more and more lately, and I have to say it's a nice change from the coffee shop's sandwiches."

"Or you could cook something yourself," Telyn pointed out. It was easier to tease and joke around than to think about what he was doing—leaving the safety of the apartment and facing the world and the people who'd been there when his mother had found him in the coffee shop.

But nothing happened. Lee and Telyn left the building, and even though Telyn felt the need to turn around and run back upstairs, he didn't. No one looked at him. No one stared. No one even noticed him, and Telyn was able to walk on, his hand linked with Lee's. The thought of food helped—he was hungry now that he wasn't afraid and worried.

"Telyn! You stop right there!"

Telyn obeyed. It was ingrained in him. He supposed he should be lucky he and Lee had managed to get to the bar parking lot. At least there, not many people would see and hear what was about to happen.

Lee had gone ramrod straight next to Telyn. "We can make a run for it, go to the bar and call the cops," he suggested.

It was tempting, but Telyn knew better than to think his mother would be deterred by it. Besides, she'd already closed in on them. The only thing they could do was face her.

Telyn turned to do just that, but to his surprise—he wasn't sure *why* he was surprised, really—Lee stepped in front of him, shielding him. "What do you want?" he asked, his voice hard. He looked uncompromising, and while Telyn knew better than to think his mother would be cowed, he was grateful.

He wanted to kiss Lee, but now wasn't the time or the place, not with his mother right there looking like she was ready to grab him and drag him home.

"Telyn. You're coming home with me, and you're coming now," Telyn's mother spat out.

"He's not going anywhere with you," Lee answered.

Telyn closed his eyes and pressed his forehead against Lee's back. He could let Lee stand in front of him and protect him like he was tempted to, or he could finally stand up to his mother and tell her exactly what he thought of her and the way she'd treated him all his life. He knew which one he wanted to do, but he also knew which one he *should* do. If he wanted to start a new life with Lee, he had to leave the past behind, and that wouldn't happen if he didn't face it.

He took a deep breath, ignored the insults that were flying between Lee and his mother, and stepped away from Lee.

Both Lee and Telyn's mother stopped talking. Telyn swallowed and finally faced the woman who'd made his life hell. "What do you want?" He was proud of the fact that his voice was steady. It wasn't as strong as he wished it was, but he was facing his mother. It was a miracle that he managed that at all.

Telyn's mother looked like she would have killed him with her eyes if it were possible. "You're coming home with me, young man."

Lee snorted, but he didn't say anything. Telyn was glad. He was letting him deal with this along with lending him support. "I *am* home," he told his mother. She opened her mouth, no doubt to protest, but he didn't give her the time. "I'm not coming back to you, and I'm not sure why you'd want me to or why you'd think I would."

"I am your mother, and you're going to listen to me."

"I'm twenty-two. I have a job, a home, and a mate. I'm not the weak demon you've always told me I was. I *left* you. I left the hell I called life, and I'm never going back to it. You should never have been allowed to have children. I should have been taken from you when I was a newborn, and the fact that I wasn't made my life horrible. But that's all in the past now. You need to leave Gillham before I ask Alpha Rhett and the police to intervene. I never want to see you again. I want to forget you exist. I want to live my life the way I want to, be happy, and that won't ever happen with you around."

Telyn didn't need to say anything more. He wasn't sure his mother would do what he was asking of her—he would have been surprised if she did without protesting—but he'd said what he wanted to say. He'd told her how bad a mother she was, and he hoped that she cared enough about him to finally leave him alone.

CHAPTER SEVEN

"Ready?" Lee could see Telyn was nervous, but he wasn't. Anyone else would have been in his place—it wasn't every day that he introduced his mate to his family and his best friend—but he already knew everything would go well. How could it not? The people he most loved in the world were finally going to meet, and there was no way they wouldn't get along.

Telyn was still staring at himself in the mirror, pulling his t-shirt down and making sure his tail was wrapped around his waist. It would be more comfortable for him while they were in the car, but Lee hoped he'd let it down once they arrived. No one would bat a lash at it, not where they were going.

"Should I tie my hair, maybe wear a hat?" Telyn asked. He pulled on a strand of his hair.

"Why would you do that?"

Telyn shrugged, but Lee could tell this was important for him. "Pink isn't a natural hair color."

"It is for you. Tel, you're not human. My family already knows that. They wouldn't expect you to die your hair a normal color even if you were, but they know you're a demon. Stop obsessing over this. They'll love you as much as I do. I promise."

Telyn glared. "You've been repeating that, but it's not helping. I can't help that I'm nervous."

Lee put his hands on Telyn's shoulders and kissed his neck. "I know. I'm trying to help, but I'll stop if you want me to shut up."

Telyn sighed. "No, I don't. I'm sorry. I'm just nervous. I don't have the best past with parents, you know."

"My parents are nothing like your mother, I promise. Come on. This can't be worse than the way *I* had to meet your mother, can it?"

Telyn laughed. He'd come a long way from that day in the parking lot a few weeks ago. They hadn't heard from his mother since then, and Lee hoped things would continue to go that way.

Telyn had been so brave, facing the woman who'd terrorized him and hurt him all his life. Lee suspected all three of them had been stunned by the way he'd stepped up to it, and Lee was so fucking proud. But Telyn finally facing his mother didn't mean he had to do it again and again, so he was glad she hadn't come back. He'd be happy if they never saw her again, and Telyn would, too. He had a new life, with a new family, and that was all he needed.

"We should go. We'll be late if we don't," Telyn said.

"You look great." Lee pushed his hips against Telyn's ass. "I wish we could stay home."

Telyn laughed. Lee hadn't been entirely serious — although he wouldn't mind spending some time in bed with Telyn — but he'd gotten what he wanted. Telyn was more relaxed, and hopefully, he'd stay that way until they got to pack territory.

Lee put some music on when they got in the car. He made sure to sing along and distract Telyn from what was waiting for them once they arrived. He might not be nervous, but he could understand why Telyn was.

"Will your brothers be there?" Telyn asked as Lee made the turn that led home.

"Yep. Brandon and Maddox, too. You can probably stick with Maddox if you're uncomfortable. He'll be as awkward as you, and he doesn't talk much."

"You said I'd be fine."

"I still think you will be, but I know you. You'll probably need some quiet time to process everything, and my family is anything but quiet."

"I suppose I should thank you for the tip, then."

"Definitely." Lee parked the car and turned the engine off. He leaned toward Telyn and kissed his cheek. "Relax, Tel. Everything's going to be fine. Even if they hate you, and they won't, it's not going to change anything between us. I love you. You're my mate. We're going to be together forever, and that's the only thing that matters."

Telyn didn't look convinced, but he didn't protest. He looked like he wouldn't have been able to talk if he tried and like he was about to throw up. That didn't get better when the front door opened before they could even get to it. Lee's mom stood there, her eyes shining, and Lee prayed she wasn't going to crowd Telyn. He'd told her and his dad about Telyn's past after getting Telyn's permission, so they knew he'd been through hell and back and that he'd probably be wary of them. Lee was pretty sure that was the only reason his mom didn't drag Telyn into a hug like she did with him.

"I need to breathe, Mom," he complained, but he hugged her back. Having his family accept Telyn was important to him, as was making sure that Telyn relaxed enough to enjoy himself.

"He's gorgeous," she murmured before letting go.

Lee shrugged. "I know. Okay, so, Telyn, this is my mom. I'm pretty sure you can call her Mom, but if that makes you uncomfortable, go with Julia. Mom, you already know this is Telyn. Please give him space. He's not used to your hugs. We don't want to have him faint right away."

Telyn's cheeks were flushed, but to Lee's surprise, he did give his mom a gentle hug. It was nothing like the one Lee and his mom had shared, but it was huge for Telyn, and Lee's heart felt like it was about to explode in his chest. He wanted to kiss his mom when she skillfully guided Telyn inside, right to the kitchen. He only got a glimpse of the others, but that was okay. Lee could introduce them once Telyn felt more comfortable.

Lee waved at his brothers, his father, Brandon, and Maddox, but he didn't stop to talk to them. He was going to stick with Telyn today. He could talk to the others next time or come on his own when Telyn was at work.

"Sit down, Telyn. Do you want a snack before lunch is ready? We still have about half an hour to go," Lee's mom said. She gestured at the stools on the other side of the counter.

Telyn looked like he'd rather do anything but sit there, but he obeyed her order and settled down. Lee hopped onto the stool next to his and grabbed his hand, squeezing until Telyn looked at him. Then he smiled, hoping he was reassuring Telyn and not freaking him out even more.

"Tell me, Telyn. What kind of demon are you? I don't know many of them, but Noah and Demi are different colors from you, and I'm curious. You can tell me to fuck off if you'd rather not answer, though."

Telyn gave Lee a startled glance, probably at the *fuck off.*

Lee chuckled. "No one here is particularly careful about the way we speak. Don't worry about it."

Telyn blinked. "I'm, uh, a madha demon."

"That's such a pretty name. Do you have a special power?"

"I see auras."

"Really?" Lee's mother put down the spoon she'd been using to mix the mashed potatoes. "It would be rude of me to ask you what you see in mine, wouldn't it?"

Telyn smiled. "Not at all. You're pink."

Lee's mom snorted. "Of course I am. I hate pink."

"It's a beautiful color, and it's streaked with silver and

green."

"What do the colors mean?"

"Pink is the color of love and tenderness. Silver means you're a nurturing person, while green means you're comfortable and happy right now."

"Oh, I like the sound of that. Your power is impressive."

Telyn blushed and looked down at the counter. "I don't know. I'm not a particularly strong reader, and there are more useful powers."

"I'm sure there are, but reading auras can be useful. You can find out what people are feeling without them talking to you."

"Ianto demons can do that, too, and probably better, since they're empaths."

Lee's mom waved. "So what? That doesn't mean you're not good at what you can do. Humans don't have any kind of power, yet they manage just fine. Think about what you could do with people who are hurt, who maybe can't or won't talk. You could help them heal. Have you thought about talking to Gentry?"

Telyn looked at Lee, obviously lost. Lee smiled and squeezed his hand. "Gentry is our psychologist. He helps people who've been through abuse and other situations to heal. Mom's not wrong, you know. You could probably help him, if that's something you want to do."

"I don't know."

Lee smiled and kissed Telyn's cheek. "Don't worry about it. You have all the time in the world to make decisions. No one is going to push you into anything." And if they tried, they'd have to answer to Lee. He was going to make sure Telyn could choose what he wanted from life without constraints or being forced into things he didn't want.

Telyn was Lee's future, and Lee was going to make sure that future was a good one, for both of them.

You may also enjoy the following from eXtasy Books Inc:

Family of the Heart
Catherine Lievens

Excerpt

Philip was doing his best not to stare, but Abel in a suit was hard to ignore. He wore it so well, and it was such a change from Abel's usually comfortable-looking clothes. It fascinated Philip, and it made him want to look even more than he normally did — which was already a lot.

At least he had something to focus on. He looked down and smiled at his son, cooing when Myron gave him a toothless smile. Myron caught Philip's finger and pulled it closer, no doubt to put it into his mouth.

"Do you want me to hold him for a bit so you can go dance?" Nico asked.

Philip shook his head. "I don't dance."

"So you can go to the bathroom, then."

"Thank you, but I'm fine."

"He meant so you can finally go talk to Abel," Nico's twin, Chris, intervened.

Philip wondered why he was sitting with them. He liked them, and most of the other carriers he was forced to live with, but sometimes they were a bit much. Maybe it was because Philip had been hidden and locked up most of his life, first by his family, then by the man who'd raped him and had killed his little girl before she even got a chance at life.

Philip swallowed. He couldn't think about that, especially not at a wedding celebration. Seamus and Alex deserved to see smiling faces around them, not Philip's horrified expression when he thought about his past. So Philip forced himself to smile. "Why should I want to talk to Abel?"

Calum snorted from the other side of the table, but he didn't say anything, and Philip was grateful for that. He was never sure how to talk to Calum, and he suspected he wasn't the only one. Calum spent most of his time in his room, and he was present tonight only because, well — Philip wasn't sure why. They hadn't been forced to attend the wedding. But Alex was a badger, and the badgers were the ones who'd offered Philip and the other carriers a safe place to stay while the council was hunting them to lock them up. Being there for Alex's wedding was a show of respect. Philip would have come just to make Seamus happy, though, and since Alex had been the one who'd rescued him from Oscar's claws, he had a special affection for him.

"Come on, Philip. Who are you trying to fool?" Chris asked.

Nico elbowed him in the ribs, but he didn't seem to care. Philip wasn't surprised. Chris was the next in line to become the alpha of his clowder, even though he was a carrier. He behaved like an alpha already, even though he was young and wouldn't take his father's place for years. He was used to people listening to him, and that hadn't changed just because he wasn't living with the clowder right now.

Philip shook his head and did his best to resist the urge to look at Abel again. "I don't know what you're talking about," he murmured.

"No? Well, I was talking about the fact that you always look at Abel like you're thirsty and he's the only one who has water."

Philip knew his cheeks were red. He could feel it.

"Or maybe he's the water," Nico mused.

Philip wanted to strangle them both. "It's not—I don't—"

He wasn't surprised when Nico reached for his arm and squeezed it. He was the sensitive twin, the one who always made sure no one got hurt by what he said or did. Chris cared, too, but he wasn't as soft and gentle as his twin. "You know we're just teasing, right?"

"Not about the way he looks at Abel," Chris said. "That shit's real, and everyone but Abel knows it."

Philips' stomach sank. "What?"

"Come on, Philip. We all have eyes, and the two of you have been dancing around each other ever since you arrived with him. He's been protective and shit, and we see the way he looks at you as well as the way you look at him."

Philip shook his head. "I'm sure you're wrong."

Chris arched a brow. "About you wanting to jump him?"

And there went Philips' cheeks again. "No." He supposed he might as well admit that. Like Chris and Nico were saying, it was obvious to most people, although Philip hoped it wasn't to Abel. He didn't know what he'd do if the man knew how he felt about him. "About him looking at me that way." Or any way.

A small commotion made the three of them look up. Several people, including Seamus, were heading inside the house. Philip wasn't sure why, but from who those people were, he could take a wild guess. They were no doubt going to talk about what was going on in the forest and how they could try dealing with the part of the council who thought carriers were nothing more than incubators for whoever paid them the most money.

"Abel's going with them," Nico noticed.

"He is a council member, you know," Chris said. "Even though he gets all soft and nice when he's with Philip." He turned back to Philip. "So? What's the problem? It's not that he's not your type, not when you look like you want to eat him up."

Goddammit. Couldn't they have stayed distracted? "He's a council member," Philip said quietly. "That means he needs someone he can take to whatever parties and dinners the council has. He needs someone he can be proud to be seen with." And that could never be Philip. Not a lot of people knew what he'd been through, but the ones who did were enough. No one had ever judged him for it, for what had been done to him, but that didn't change the fact that it had tainted him.

He looked down at Myron. He loved his son with all his being, and he always would. That didn't change the way he was conceived, though. It didn't matter to Philip, but it would to other people, and no matter how gentle Abel was, he had to deal with those people. It was his job.

"Oh, no," Nico snapped.

That was so unusual for him that Philip blinked at him. "What?"

"You're not thinking what I think you're thinking, are you?"

"I have no idea. I can't read your mind."

Nico's eyes narrowed. "You are good enough. Abel would be proud to be seen with you. I know it. He's a good man."

"I know." Philip kept his gaze down. He didn't want to face Chris and Nico.

"Then what's the problem?"

"He wouldn't care, but what about everyone else?" And even knowing Abel didn't mind Philip's past, it was hard to believe he might want Philip the way Philip wanted him. Like Nico said, he was a good man, and that was probably the reason he was always so sweet and gentle. He knew what Philip had gone through and didn't want him to be hurt again. That was why he was so careful. It had to be.

"They can go fuck themselves," Chris said.

That startled a laugh out of Philip. "I'm not surprised that's what you think." After all, he was probably used to tongues wagging about him. He was the heir to his clowder, and he was a carrier. A carrier had never been an alpha. Philip still wasn't sure it would happen, not with the way things were in the forest right now, but if there was anyone who could face the council and win this battle, it was Chris.

"It's not that simple," Philip tried to explain.

Chris snorted. "Yeah, it is. You want him, and he wants you. That's the only two people you need to think of. Well, and Myron, but he doesn't count since he doesn't have an opinion yet. He could do with a second dad, though, and so could you. You look like you're about to fall asleep on your plate."

Philip frowned. "That's because Myron still feeds at night."

"I know. I wasn't blaming you or anything. I just think it's stupid that you're letting what other people think stop you from being happy. I might be able to understand that if we were talking about your family, but we're not. The people who might have something to say about your relationship with Abel are assholes, so what do you care about then? Abel would be lucky to have you in his life like that. Being a carrier doesn't make you less of a person."

"I know that." But no matter what Chris thought, what other people would say did count. Abel's job with the council depended on it.

About the Author

Catherine lives in Italy, country of good food and hot men. She used to write fantasy as a child, but it was reading her first gay erotic romance novel that made her realize that that was what she really wanted to write.

After graduating from college in English language and translation, she divides her day between writing, reading, taking care of her son and reading some more.

You can find her on Facebook and Twitter or on her website: authorcatherinelievens.wordpress.com

Email: lievens.catherine@gmail.com

Newsletter: http://eepurl.com/c-uvKn

www.ingramcontent.com/pod-product-compliance
Lightning Source LLC
Chambersburg PA
CBHW060633130626

46555CB00002B/779